Introduction

Where to begin? *First Contact* is just that, a place for readers, be they teen or adult, to make a first foray into the world of science fiction and fantasy. The categories and novels are our own favorites; note that science fiction and fantasy titles are mixed in each chapter. There are classics in each category as well as current titles popular with both younger and older teens. The designations **M**, **J**, **S** or combinations thereof, stand for middle school, grades 6–8; junior high school, grades 7–9; and senior high school, grades 10–12, respectively. We hope that reading some of these favorite novels will begin your enchantment with both science fiction and fantasy. Rather than a comprehensive selection tool, this volume is a beginning reader's advisory book, a key to unlock the delicious array of imaginative writing in these challenging genres.

First Contact

A Reader's Selection
of Science Fiction and Fantasy

Bonnie Kunzel
Suzanne Manczuk

The Scarecrow Press, Inc.
Lanham, Maryland, and London
2001

SCARECROW PRESS, INC.

Published in the United States of America
by Scarecrow Press, Inc.
4720 Boston Way
Lanham, Maryland 20706
www.scarecrowpress.com

4 Pleydell Gardens, Folkestone
Kent CT20 2DN, England

British Library Cataloguing-in-Publication Information Available

Library of Congress Cataloging-in-Publication Data

Kunzel, Bonnie, 1944–
    First contact : a reader's selection of science fiction and fantasy / Bonnie Kunzel and Suzanne
    Manczuk.
        p. cm.
    Includes bibliographical references and index.
    ISBN 0-8108-4028-6 (pbk. : alk. paper)
    1. Science fiction, American—Bibliography. 2. Children's stories, American—Stories, plots,
etc. 3. Children's stories, English—Stories, plots, etc. 4. Science fiction, American—Stories,
plots, etc. 5. Fantasy fiction, American—Stories, plots, etc. 6. Children's stories, American—
Bibliography. 7. Children's, stories, English—Bibliography. 8. Fantasy fiction, American—
Bibliography. 9. Science fiction, English—Bibliography. 10. Fantasy fiction, English—
Bibliography. [1. Science fiction—Bibliography. 2. Fantasy—Bibliography.] I. Manczuk,
Suzanne, 1945– . II. Title.
Z1231.F4K86 2001
[PS374.S35]
016.813'087608—dc21   2001020300

For Dorothy and Mary K.

Contents

Acknowledgments

We would like to thank Dorothy Broderick and Mary K. Chelton for inspiration, encouragement, and friendship; and our husbands, George and Joe, for their understanding of the true meaning of "partner" and "helpmate."

Alien Contact

What species exist in the universe, and what will happen when earthlings encounter new life-forms? Meeting alien beings can be a peaceful experience, or it can be an invitation to conflict, all-out war, or annihilation.

1. Brin, David. *Startide Rising*. Bantam Books, 1983. **J S**
Sentient species have been uplifted to space-faring status all through the galaxy. In exchange, they must serve as virtual slaves to the patron races that sponsored them. The wolflings of Earth are the exception. They achieved space flight themselves without a patron and in turn have uplifted the apes and the dolphins. When the dolphin ship *Streaker* discovers the remains of a flotilla that belonged to the mysterious progenitors, the other patron races want the discovery for themselves and move in for the kill. What they haven't counted on is the fierce struggle they will face from the uplifted Earth species. Sequels: *The Uplift War*; *Brightness Reef*; *Infinity's Shore*; *Heaven's Reach*. Prequel: *Sundiver*.

2. Card, Orson Scott. *Ender's Game*. Tor, 1992. **M J S**
Ender Wiggins was just a child when he was taken away from his parents by the government and placed in a special school. There, he and other gifted children were trained to fight against alien invaders, though they thought they were just playing computer games. When the war was over, Ender learned that his final battle against the Buggers and their hive queen was much more than just a game. Sequels: *Speaker for the Dead*; *Xenocide*; *Children of the Mind*. Companion novels: *Ender's Shadow*; *Shadow of the Hegemon*.

3. Cherryh, C. J. *Foreigner: A Novel of First Contact*. Daw Books, 1995. **S**
Bren Cameron is the official ambassador to the Atevi and as such is the

only human allowed to make direct contact with them since the end of the human/Atevi wars. When an assassination attempt leaves Bren running for his life, it is the members of his Atevi bodyguard who are his only hope of escape. The question is—how long can this foreigner trust his life to representatives of a race that have very different concepts of truth and friendship and do not even understand the meaning of the word "like"? Sequels: *Invader*; *Inheritor*; *Precursor*.

4. Christopher, John. *The White Mountains*. Simon & Schuster, 1987. **M J**
Book One of the Tripods Trilogy introduces Will Parker. At thirteen, Will is one year short of the Capping ceremony performed on all fourteen-year-olds by the Tripods. While most of the capped are happy and serve their masters faithfully, they have lost all initiative and drive as a result of the ceremony. An unfortunate few suffer an adverse reaction and become Vagrants, people mentally burned out, aimlessly wandering through the countryside. A man disguised as a Vagrant tells Will how to avoid being capped: he must flee before the ceremony, make his way to the White Mountains, and join the uncapped resistance force there in its struggle against the Tripods. Sequels: *The City of Gold and Lead*; *The Pool of Fire*. Prequel: *When the Tripods Came*.

5. Clarke, Arthur C. *Childhood's End*. Harcourt, 1963. **M J S**
In a novel acknowledged by many to be one of this author's best works, alien spaceships arrive in the skies above Earth. The satanic-looking beings inside them are on a mission to save humanity. Their goal is to help the children of Earth cast off the restraints that have hobbled their parents and successfully make the passage to the next stage of human evolution.

6. Crispin, A. C. *Starbridge*. Ace Books, 1989. **M J S**
As a teenage colonist going to Earth on her aunt and uncle's spaceship to continue her education, Mahree Burroughs keeps a diary that becomes a record of humanity's first contact with an alien species. When her ship picks up a radio transmission in space and tracks it to its source, humans come face to face with the Simiu for the first time. Mahree is the first to befriend a Simiu, the young male Dhurrrkk, and it is their relationship that leads ultimately to cooperation between the two species. This is the first in a series that explores cooperation among sentient beings and establishes Starbridge Academy as a place of learning for the young of all species. Sequels: *Silent Dances*; *Shadow World*; *Serpent's Gift* (with Deborah A. Marshall); *Silent Songs* (with Kathleen O'Malley).

7. Dexter, Catherine. *Alien Game*. William Morrow, 1995. **M J**
Eighth grader Zoe Brook is getting ready for her school's annual elimination game. Teachers as well as students participate in a modified version of Gotcha, with anyone caught walking alone fair game. Zoe isn't all that enthusiastic about playing this year until the mysterious new girl in school lets everyone know she can't wait. Just after Zoe learns about the class that disappeared years ago while playing the game, she sees the new girl turn into a swarm of fireflies while standing at her locker. What does that mean about this year's game and who will survive?

8. Foster, Alan Dean. *For Love of Mother-Not*. Severn House Publishers, 1993. **M J S**
Flinx was only eight years old when Mother Mastiff bought him in the slave market. Shortly afterward, he found Pip, a minidragon, in the garbage. Flinx knows nothing about his past, nothing about being created by the Meliorites in an effort to improve upon humanity. He also doesn't know that his special talents are much stronger now because the minidragon Pip is a catalyst animal. Once the two are bonded, Flinx's ability to read and manipulate the emotions of those around him is enhanced. After they find him when he is sixteen, the Meliorites want their empathic telepath back, and they try to control him by kidnapping his adoptive mother (whom he calls his Mother-Not). The Meliorites soon discover, however, that it was a big mistake to make an enhanced Flinx mad. This is the first in a series about the adventures of Flinx and his minidragon Pip. Sequels: *The Tar-Aiym Krang*; *Orphan Star*; *The End of the Matter*; *Bloodhype*; *Flinx in Flux*; *Mid-Flinx*.

9. Gilmore, Kate. *The Exchange Student*. Houghton Mifflin, 1999. **M J**
Not your ordinary exchange student, Fen is from the planet Chela. Daria's family takes in the odd-looking alien (Fen changes colors, is abnormally tall and thin, and there are those pointy teeth!). It is up to teenager Daria, animal lover and biology student, to help the alien adjust to his Earth stay. Daria keeps a menagerie of animals in a laboratory, determined to aid in the restoration of Earth's animal species. Fen is fascinated by animals. Gilmore sets up the mystery of why the Chelans (yes, there are others) came to Earth in the first place—they so obviously are concealing something.

10. Harrison, Harry. *Deathworld*. Bantam Books, 1960. **J S**
Jason dinAlt is a man with a problem. He has been sent to the Deathworld, a planet where every life form is a deadly threat to human settlers.

Fortunately, Jason has enough firepower and the fast reaction time to use it in an endless series of battles for existence. And there's no guarantee that survival of the fittest refers to Jason and the other humans on the planet. Sequels: *Deathworld 2*; *Deathworld 3*.

11. Heald, Denise Lopes. *Mistwalker*. Ballantine/Del Rey, 1994. **S**
Sal is a sled-hauler, trying to make a living by hauling supplies through the jungle on a planet where an encounter with Mistwalkers usually means death. Meesha Raschad is a newbie, or newcomer to the planet. He did not die in his first encounter with the Mistwalkers; instead he developed a special immunity to them. When the two become partners, it is not only the terrors in the jungle they must overcome but also the unscrupulous government forces working against them.

12. Heinlein, Robert A. *Stranger in a Strange Land*. Penguin Putnam, 1976. **S**
The stranger is Valentine Michael Smith, a young Earthman raised by Martians. The strange land is the Earth to which he has returned, bringing with him paranormal powers gained during his stay on Mars. A cult favorite as well as a Hugo-winner, this novel introduced the term "grokking" and espoused both free love and the mystical beliefs of its Messiah-like protagonist who chooses to discorporate himself at the end.

13. Klause, Annette Curtis. *Alien Secrets*. Bantam Doubleday Dell, 1993. **M J**
Puck is on her way home to Aurora in disgrace, since she was kicked out of boarding school for her poor grades and for getting into trouble. Her parents' research on Aurora involves the alien Shoowa, and as luck would have it, a fellow passenger on her spaceship is a Shoowa. In fact, Hush is the first of his species to return to Aurora since the tyrannical Grakk enslaved them years ago. Unfortunately, Hush was robbed of an artifact of major importance to his people, and it may now be somewhere aboard ship. Puck puts her life in danger by helping Hush search for the missing artifact.

14. McCaffrey, Anne. *Freedom's Landing*. Putnam Penguin, 1995. **J S**
Aliens invaded Earth and took the inhabitants of various cities away with them to a life of slavery among the stars. Kristin Bjornsen is one of these slaves, but she manages to escape her Catteni master and hide in the wilderness for five months. When she sees Zainal, a Catteni chased by others of his own kind, she helps him escape. Returning with him to the city is a mistake because he has enemies still trying to get

rid of him. The two are captured and are put on a spaceship that is part of Operation Fresh Start. Along with other settlers, they are dropped on a beautiful green planet where strange machines and even stranger farming techniques are still very much in operation. This planet was settled and then abandoned by the mysterious Mech Makers, but the settlers soon discover to their peril that they have not forgotten it. Sequels: *Freedom's Choice*; *Freedom's Challenge*.

15. Niven, Larry and Jerry Pournelle. *The Mote in God's Eye*. Simon & Schuster, 1974. **S**
The aliens are coming! When they arrive, the galactic aristocracies discover just how powerful a threat they are to the continued existence of the new empire. A large cast of characters refuses to believe that resistance is futile in an epic best-seller that is full of imaginative twists and turns.

16. Nix, Garth. *Shade's Children*. HarperCollins, 1997. **J S**
Since The Change, life has been violent and bleak for the children of Earth. Herded into the Dorms until age fourteen, teens are then sent to the Meat Factory to become body parts for evil creatures, losing their human brains and muscles to the Overlord's hunters—the flying wingers, earthbound trackers, nighttime ferrets, and gigantic Myrmidons. Four teens who have managed to escape the Dorms and the gory Meat Factory—Ella, Gold Eye, Drum, and Ninde—bond together. Their benefactor, Shade, leads them in a fierce battle against the seemingly omnipotent Overlords. Author Nix weaves together the four teens' individual stories, concealing Shade's identity until late in the plot, and finishing with a battle of wits and firepower between Shade's children and the Overlords.

17. Norton, Andre. *Brother to Shadows*. William Morrow, 1993. **S**
Jofre is an offworlder adopted into a lair of assassins as a young boy and trained by its master. When the lair's force stone dies, Jofre is cast out to die. Instead, he picks up special powers from the force stone of another long-dead lair. Afterward, Jofre goes to work for Zurzal, a Zacathan scholar needing help with his project of bringing the past to life. The Thieves Guild is interested in Zurzal's work and wants Jofre, dead or alive. But Jofre has a new ally, a lovable, furry little creature named Yan that has enhanced his powers and warns him telepathically of danger. A civil war, assassination attempts, and kidnapping are only some of the dangers Jofre faces in his quest for the Forerunners and what

they left behind. Prequels: *Storm over Warlock*; *Ordeal in Otherwhere*; *Forerunner Foray*; *Forerunner*; *Forerunner: The Second Venture*.

18. Pratchett, Terry. *Truckers*. Delacorte Press, 1991. **M J**
    Four-inch high Nomes were stranded on Earth some fifteen thousand years ago. But with the passage of centuries, they have forgotten their offworld heritage. Masklin's group, with only ten surviving members, now lives a hand-to-mouth existence near a diner. When it becomes obvious they will not survive another winter, Masklin talks them into stowing away on a truck. When the truck delivers them to the store, their arrival is a shock to the two thousand Nomes living there. Until these newcomers showed up, the store Nomes had believed that there was no such thing as the outside. Shortly after his arrival, Masklin discovers that the store will be demolished in just twenty-one days. All the Nomes are doomed unless Masklin can get them to follow his plans for their evacuation by becoming truckers. Sequels: *Diggers*; *Wings*.

19. Rubinstein, Gillian. *Galax-Arena*. Simon & Schuster, 1995. **M J**
    The children Joella, Peter, and Liane are drugged, kidnapped, and spirited away by rocket ship to the planet Vexak to become performers in the Galax-Arena. In the gymnastic training school for the peb, the children learn that not all are suited for the Galax-Arena and that some become caged pets for the dreaded Vexa. Rubinstein cleverly opens her tale with the three children back on Earth, so the reader puzzles out how and why an escape from the planet occurred.

20. Shusterman, Neal. *The Dark Side of Nowhere*. Little, Brown, 1996. **M J**
    Billington seems an average American town, and Jason Miller seems to come from a nice, normal family. The only strange event in Jason's life is his monthly visit to a doctor for shots. When the young teen Ethan dies, supposedly from appendicitis, Jason's curiosity is roused. It also seems strange to him that there is no information in the local library from the year 1976. But it is Mr. Grant with the shooting gray glove who is the strangest of all, and when Jason begins to question his parents about events, they inform him that they are not of Earth but came from another planet. Is there a ship on its way from outer space, a ship that Jason, his parents, and the other aliens have long awaited? Shusterman spins an intriguing tale of alien life hiding in human bodies.

21. Silverberg, Robert. *The Alien Years*. HarperCollins, 1998. **S**
    The aliens came to Earth and conquered it with very little effective re-

sistance. Humankind survived and attempted to fight back against impossible odds and incredible indifference on the part of the aliens, fifteen-feet tall purple squids. The resistance effort is led by Colonel Carmichael, patriarch of a family that fights the entities for decades, but to no avail. The aliens are either hideously ugly or indescribably beautiful, depending on the eye of the beholder and whether or not that person has been mentally manipulated by the aliens and their telepathic push. The Carmichaels turn their family farm in the Santa Barbara hills into an armed enclave and fight the good fight for generations. The aliens never say why they came or what they want. They simply remain an immovable force, for as long as they want to, leaving humans to discover that resistance really is futile.

22. Sleator, William. *Interstellar Pig*. Dutton, 1984. **M J**
Barney and his parents are spending a quiet, relaxing, and for Barney, incredibly boring vacation at the beach. The new tenants next door soon change all of that. They invite Barney to join them in a game of Interstellar Pig, a game for possession of the Piggy and protection from annihilation. Barney has a wonderful time until he discovers that the Piggy and the game are both real and that the fate of Earth is hanging in the balance.

23. Wells, H. G. *The War of the Worlds*. William Heineman, 1898. **M J S**
A classic tale of BEMs, that is, bug-eyed monsters. The Martians have landed on Earth, and life as it is known is in danger. They descend upon London, protected from attack inside three-legged machines that shoot out heat rays. There is no hope for Earth . . . or is there? Americans ran for their lives in 1938 when Orson Welles and Howard Koch turned this novel into a radio play, with the Martians landing in New Jersey and causing widespread riot.

24. Wyndham, John. *The Day of the Triffids*. Del Rey, 1951. **M J S**
Mysterious explosions blind almost the entire human race. These explosions are followed by the sudden appearance of giant triffids, walking plants with deadly stingers that attack humans, easy prey now that they are blind. Those few who can still see lead the battle against these deadly plants for the survival of humankind.

All Creatures Great and Small

Human beings are fascinated by the idea that animal communities might have their own particular civilizations. In these novels, rabbits, badgers, foxes, and bees, among other fauna, operate in their own societies, which oftentimes bear a remarkable resemblance to the human world.

25. Adams, Richard. *Watership Down*. Macmillan, 1974. **M J S**
    A premonition of blood and death sends a plucky band of adventurers off on an epic quest. These seekers are rabbits, however, not humans, led by Hazel with dreamer Fiver among them, searching for a safe warren and company to join their small band of travelers. The tale of the journey is sprinkled with rabbit mythology and lore, especially the lessons of the rabbit folk hero El Ahrairah. No quiet bunny story, *Watership Down* takes its place as a classic animal fantasy adventure, one that, to date, has no sequel and few equals.

26. Avi. *Perloo the Bold*. Scholastic, 1998. **M**
    "Knowing the length of a Montmer's ear won't tell you if he can listen."
    "Only the dead have no choices."
    "The future begins in the past."
    Words of wisdom from Mogwat the magpie, friend and prophet to the community of Montmers—fantasy creatures that visibly look a little rabbitty but that have their own peculiar physical attributes. The reluctant hero, Perloo, living apart from the Central Tribe Burrow, is summoned by the dying Granter Jolaine. Jolaine has the power to appoint her successor, but in her weakened state, she cannot rally against her arrogant child, Berwig. The stage is set for a grand battle for the Burrow, with Perloo sidestepping Grantership all the way. A fine parable

of a tale that explores the giving and receiving of power, the value of friendship, and the nature of war.

27. Bakker, Robert T. *Raptor Red*. Bantam Books, 1995. **J S**
The narrator is a female raptor who lived in prehistoric Utah 120 million years ago, and this is one year in her life, beginning with the tragic death of her mate. Fortunately, she meets her sister and her three chicks, thereby increasing her chances of survival. Together they hunt iguanodons, face storms and a flash flood, and are forced to migrate to escape powerful predators. Through it all, Raptor Red's biological clock is ticking, driving her to find a new mate and reproduce before it is too late.

28. Bell, Clare. *Ratha's Challenge*. Simon & Schuster, 1983. **M J**
This is the fourth in the series about Ratha, a great cat gifted with the ability to talk. It features her daughter, Thistle-Chaser, whom Ratha drove away from the Clan years ago because she mistakenly believed that her daughter did not have the ability to talk. It is fortunate that they have since reconciled, for both are needed when the Clan's attempt to capture facetails (mammoths) leads to a confrontation with a different tribe of great cats. These strangers can talk in the same way that Ratha's tribe can, but they also can communicate by means of a mental song that only Thistle can hear. With her special talents, it is Thistle who will bring the tribes together, if she doesn't die in the attempt. Prequels: *Ratha's Creature*; *Clan Ground*; *Ratha and Thistle-Chaser*.

29. Clement, Aeron. *The Cold Moons*. Kindredsen, 1987. **M J S**
Disease is attacking the badgers in sets of southwestern England and Wales—are the badgers carrying tuberculosis and infecting the local cattle? Or is it the other way around? Whichever the case, the badger Bamber makes an arduous journey from Yellow Copse to Cilgwyn to warn his fellow creatures of the coming dangers. In the tradition of *Watership Down*, *The Cold Moons* chronicles the epic struggle of the badger species to find a safe haven and to live their lives in peace and contentment.

30. Foster, Alan Dean. *Dinotopia Lost*. HarperCollins, 1998. **J S**
This is a full-length novel set in the lost world of Dinotopia created by James Gurney. Will Denison, the teenage son of scientist Arthur Denison, was marooned on the island with his father years ago. Now he must rescue a dinosaur family in peril. Pirates, stranded on the island by a storm, have begun capturing dinosaurs to take back to civilization.

Will is on their trail, but these pirates have made a really big mistake—they have taken their captives into the Rainy Basin, home of the tyrannosaurs, and added a baby tyrannosaur to their collection. The storm of the century is headed for the island, but Will is less worried about that than what will happen if the baby's parents get to the pirates before he does. Sequel: *The Hand of Dinotopia*; Prequels (by James Gurney): *Dinotopia: A Land Apart from Time*; *Dinotopia: The World Beneath*; *Dinotopia: First Flight*.

31. Friesner, Esther. *Majyk by Accident*. Ace Books, 1993. **S**
Thengor, master of the School for Wizards, is dying. This means that all of his Majyk will soon be available for the taking. Thengor wants to pass it on to his chosen heir and the best student in the school, Zoltan Fiendlord, but fate intervenes in the form of Kendar Ratwhacker, that most inept and clumsy student who still doesn't even have his first robe after six years of study. Stationed beside a rat hole with his cudgel, Kendar is startled when a funny-looking creature emerges. With a plaintive "Meow," the creature darts past Kendar and runs across the wizard's deathbed. Kendar is in hot pursuit, but when he runs through the master's Majyk aura, it immediately attaches itself to him. In a hilarious set of misadventures, Kendar and the cat go on the run, trying to escape from Fiendlord and the other wizards who will do anything to get their master's Majyk back—up to and including murder. Sequel: *By Hook or By Crook*.

32. Hawdon, Robin. *A Rustle in the Grass*. Dodd, Mead, 1984. **M J S**
Fans of *Watership Down* will enjoy this novel that depicts the struggle for survival of a colony of ants. Faced with the threat of invasion by vicious red ants, the leaders of the colony send Dreamer to investigate. This young ant gets his name from the strange dreams he has of events about to unfold. He is also known as Quick Feelers because he has such long feelers that he is able to sense things further away and more quickly than his fellow ants. Dreamer is captured by enemy ants but manages to escape and return with a warning. He then plays a major role in the final rousing battle.

33. Jacques, Brian. *Redwall*. Philomel, 1986. **M J S**
Cluny the Scourge and his coterie of weasels, rats, and evil fellows are marching through Mossflower Wood toward the gentle haven of Redwall Abbey. Can Abbott Mortimer, Constance the badger, and the young mouse Mathias thwart this band of cutthroats that threaten the tranquility

of the Abbey residents? In this first of thirteen-going-on-fourteen tales of Redwall, the stage is set for the continuing battles between the good and evil creatures that inhabit Jacques's very popular series. Not for the squeamish—battles gory and bloody abound—these lengthy stories are also filled with challenging dialect and constant culinary delights. A feast for the fans. The series to date: *Mossflower*; *Mattimeo*; *Mariel of Redwall*; *Salamandastron*; *Martin the Warrior*; *The Bellmaker*; *Outcast of Redwall*; *The Great Redwall Feast* (picture book); *The Pearls of Lutra*; *The Long Patrol*; *Marlfox*; *The Legend of Luke*; *Lord Brocktree*.

34. Kilworth, Garry. *The Foxes of First Dark*. Doubleday, 1990. **J S**
O-ha the vixen is secure in her sanctuary of Trinity Woods, mating with the handsome A-ho and patiently waiting for her cubs to be born. Rumors filter through Trinity that evil humans will take over the woodland community, forcing the animal life to flee to safer territory. When A-ho is brutally murdered, O-ha is shocked into searching for both a new home and a new mate that will offer her some protection from human encroachment. Kilworth's allegorical fantasy poses age-old questions to readers: Does one choose safe havens over exciting possibilities? Can the weak successfully conquer the powerful? And what does one sacrifice for the safety of one's children? A detailed and fluidly written story with unforgettable characters.

35. Lally, Soinbhe. *A Hive for the Honeybee*. Scholastic, 1990. **J S**
Thora and Belle are worker bees in their hive. Alfred, a drone, is the hive's poet laureate, and Mo, another drone, is a questioning male bee. Together these four begin to unravel the strict rules of the honeybee community, doubting whether living life as a useless drone (except for the one moment of purpose, mating with the queen), or as a mindless worker is all there is to a full existence. Lally spins an allegory that questions government control, the role of women, and even religion in a society. While fantastic in some elements, the tale sticks closely to the zoological facts of bee culture.

36. Oppel, Kenneth. *Silverwing*. Simon & Schuster, 1997. **M**
Runt. Pipsqueak. Shade is the smallest of the young bats of Tree Haven, the ultimate outsider and the object of bigger bats' constant teasing. Just before the colony's winter migration to Hibernaculum, Shade breaks a sacred bat rule: when the dawn chorus sings, bats must return to the colony, never staying out to look at the sun. His foolish bravado brings disaster upon the haven, and tiny Shade is separated

from the bats during the arduous migration. Shade is determined to find his family. His adventures include an episode with the gigantic vampire bat, Goth—an appropriately gruesome chapter. Readers will be pulling for this miniature creature, identifying with Shade's oh-so-adolescent struggle to find his place in the community and prove his worthiness to family and friends. Sequel: *Sunwing*

37. Wangerin, Walter Jr. *The Book of the Dun Cow*. HarperCollins, 1978. **M J S**
In this stylized allegorical fantasy, Chauntecleer the rooster, leader of the animal world, faces a malevolent evil that is threatening to obliterate the peace and goodness of God's creation. Peopled with animal characters such as John Wesley Weasel and Mundo Cani Dog, Wangerin's dark and elegant tale is laced with violence and concludes with a bloody battle between the satanic Wyrm and the good creatures of Chauntecleer's Coop.

38. Werber, Bernard. *Empire of the Ants*. Bantam Books, 1998. **S**
"Never go down into the cellar": an ominous warning for Jonathan Wells and his Parisian family when they inherit eccentric Uncle Edmond's flat. After the family dog disappears down the cellar steps, Jonathan, wife, and son do enter the treacherous underworld, with bizarre consequences to follow. Parallel to this mysterious human drama is the story of a nearby ant civilization where the russet colony of Bel-o-kan is in conflict with warring neighbor ants. As usual in animal fantasies, this ant world faces annihilation from the world of humans. Alternating the voices of ant and human characters, Werber cleverly draws the reader into this sometimes warped and savage story. Though the ants' tale is more intriguing than the people's narrative, *Empire* hooks readers with unusual characters and heaps of gore in the battle scenes.

Alternate Reality

Might there be another world out there, a parallel universe? Characters in these stories discover worlds similar to Earth, or even on Earth, but these worlds function separately from ordinary human history as we know it.

39. Aiken, Joan. *Is Underground*. Delacorte Press, 1993. **M J**
Plucky heroine Is Twite sets out for London to find her missing cousin, Arun. Once in the bustling nineteenth-century city, her search unravels a curious tale of many missing children, including the king's own son. Nefarious adults are luring children to the Playland Express, a train that travels north to coal country, whereupon arriving, the young mysteriously disappear. Determined to restore Arun to his family, Is bravely follows the path of the kidnapped boys and girls, using her wit and keen intelligence to solve the dastardly crimes. Sequel: *Cold Shoulder Road*.

40. Anderson, Kevin J. and John Gregory Betancourt. *Born of Elven Blood*. Simon & Schuster, 1995. **J S**
Sixteen-year-old Maria is saved from a mugger by a young man that guides her through a heavy mist into the Faery realm. Prince Cyn then explains that he needs her to help him warn the king that the trogs are active again and war is imminent. He assures her that he will return her to her own world before her mother misses her so she can relax and enjoy a storybook adventure. Unfortunately it is an adventure that ends in tragedy, requiring a heroic sacrifice to stop the war and opening a permanent gateway between Faery- and humankind. Another entry in the *Dragonflight* series that features original fantasies for teen readers.

41. Bova, Ben. *Triumph*. TOR Books, 1992. **J S**
What would have happened if World War II had turned out differently?
Suppose President Roosevelt had stopped smoking, did not have a fatal stroke, and remained healthy and fully in charge. Suppose Winston
Churchill was convinced that Stalin would become a dangerous beast
and took steps to eradicate him before the end of the war. Suppose Patton pushed through to Berlin and arrived before the Russians. And suppose that America became the only game in town, a worldwide empire
that kept atomic weaponry out of the hands of all other nations.

42. Card, Orson Scott. *Seventh Son*. TOR Books, 1987. **J S**
Alvin Maker is a very special child: the seventh son of a seventh son.
Although he is the beloved of Earth, Air, and Fire, he must maintain
constant vigilance against the dangers he faces from Water. The family
moves west and his childhood is a happy one until his father begins to
have irrational fits, during which he is commanded to kill his son.
Eventually, Alvin must leave home if he hopes to survive long enough
to grow up and learn how to use his mystical abilities. Sequels: *Red
Prophet*; *Prentice Alvin*; *Alvin Journeyman*; *Heartfire: The Tales of
Alvin Maker V*.

43. De Lint, Charles. *Memory and Dream*. TOR Books, 1994. **S**
Izzy is a talented artist who falls under the spell of the wrong man.
Rushkin senses that Izzy has the ability to imbue life in her artistic creations. A master artist in his own right, he nurtures Izzy's craft and
teaches her how to create Gateway Portraits of the denizens of Faerie.
He then watches closely as she brings these subjects across to their
world. What she doesn't find out until it's almost too late is that he
feeds upon her creations, thereby extending his own life. When Izzy
falls in love with one of her creations and tries to fight back, Rushkin
is ready to sacrifice the artist as well to his voracious appetite.

44. De Lint, Charles. *Trader*. TOR Books, 1996. **S**
Max Trader wakes up one morning in a strange room and in a strange
body. He knows who he is: the talented and widely respected luthier
Max Trader. But when he looks in the mirror, he sees the face of a
stranger, that of a much younger and handsomer man. He soon discovers who this man is—the lazy, shiftless, womanizing ne'er-do-well
Johnny Devlin. Max finds Johnny living in his house and discovers that
he is living in Johnny's; when he demands that they swap back,
Johnny, who now has access to Max's shop and bank account, refuses.

Before long, poor Max finds himself evicted from Johnny's apartment, roaming the streets. He wonders what has happened to him, why the change took place, and most important of all, how it can be reversed. He finds the solution in the prophecy of a Native American fortune-teller that will lead him to a final confrontation with Johnny in the spirit world. Once again, Charles De Lint uses his powerful imagination to take the reader on a memorable excursion into the world of Faerie.

45. DuBois, Brendan. *Resurrection Day*. Putnam, 1999. **S**
   This apocalyptic "what if" thriller features a United States in which the Bay of Pigs fiasco, the discovery of nukes in Cuba, and the blockade of Russian ships led to a nuclear exchange between Russia and the United States that destroyed all the major cities in both countries. It is ten years after the bombs fell, and the United States has been reduced to the level of a third-world country. Carl Landry, a former special forces veteran, working as a reporter for the *Boston Globe,* investigates the murder of another veteran, but then the military censors won't let him print anything about it in the paper. Next someone tries to kill him at the same time that he hears a rumor that England is planning to invade the United States. The result is a riveting, fast-paced thriller that packs quite a punch.

46. Gould, Stephen. *Wildside*. TOR Books, 1996. **S**
   What if a parallel world existed? A world unspoiled by pollution, government intervention, or even human habitation? Eighteen-year-old Charlie Newell inherits such a world from his Uncle Max, and all is idyllic while Charlie and his friends explore this new planet—until the United States government, the FBI, and other interested parties begin to chase Charlie. Clever and suspenseful plotting with teen protagonists center stage.

47. Jones, Diana Wynne. *Hexwood*. Greenwillow Books, 1994. **J S**
   Time, place, people, and events are at their most baffling in Jones's quixotic puzzle-novel about Hexwood farm in a story that challenges the reader to sort out an intricate and multilayered plot. The catalyst is twelve-year-old Ann, greengrocer's daughter, avid reader, and curious observer of the country property Hexwood. Vehicles pull up to the Farm's gate, go into the woods, and seem never to come out. Ann's curiosity leads her to enter this frightening world that expands across time and space to include Arthurian Britain and

the wide galaxies of the future universe. With an ancient machine called the Bannus, the skull-faced creature Mordion, and five galactic lords known as the Reigners, Jones dazzles the reader with her brilliant (though sometimes confusing) plot. An intellectually challenging read.

48. Kleier, Glen. *The Last Day*. Warner Books, 1997. **S**
    As the world approaches the final days of 1999, fears abound of an apocalyptic end to the millennium. On New Year's Eve, 1999, a strange young woman named Jeza appears in the Negev Desert. Is she Messiah? Antichrist? A hoax? The established church fears and resents her, cult followers worship her, and the veteran news media is skeptical of her message. TV reporter Jon Feldman follows the preacher Jeza, beginning his media coverage in complete disbelief and ending in the year 2000 with more questions than he can answer. Packed with action, plot reversals, and the riveting central figure of Jeza herself, millennium fever doesn't get any better treatment than Kleier's novel.

49. Lethem, Jonathan. *Gun, with Occasional Music*. Harcourt, 1994. **S**
    Conrad Metcalf, like everyone else in Oakland, has a drug dependency, but that doesn't keep him from doing his job as a private investigator. He left the Inquisitors and took up private practice when he could no longer stomach the group's rough-and-ready system of dispensing justice. His latest client is scheduled to be frozen by the Inquisition for a murder that he did not commit. Once Metcalf begins investigating, a trigger-happy kangaroo gets on his trail, proof positive that evolution therapy is not always such a good idea. When an underworld figure also gets involved, it's no longer just Metcalf's client who is being threatened with the freezer.

50. Levy, Robert. *Escape from Exile*. Houghton Mifflin, 1993. **M J**
    While trying to get home through a snowstorm to his younger sister, Daniel gets lost, is zapped by Z-shaped lightning, and wakes up on another world just in time to save a vicious catlike tomago from a trap. Discovering that he can talk to the animals on this world, Daniel befriends a horse-like mahemuth and a small but deadly snake. Not until he meets the samkits, though, does he find out why and how he has been transported to Lithia. There is a struggle going on for the crown, and Daniel gets involved by befriending the evil king's ten-year-old daughter. Through it all, he never loses sight of his need to return home and the younger sister waiting for him.

51. Norton, Andre and Rosemary Edghill. *The Shadow of Albion. Carolus Rex: Book I.* TOR Books, 1999. **S**
Sorcery, witchcraft, and a Regency romance are all rolled into one in this diverting fantasy romp. In an alternative history, England is ruled not by the Catholic James and his narrow-minded followers but by the duke of Monmouth, true heir to Charles II. France has a strong, imperial Napoleon Bonaparte, and the New World has never rebelled but remains the westernmost of England's possessions. It is from the New World that the destitute Sarah Cunningham comes to England in 1805 at the behest of the ancient dowager duchess of Wessex to right an ancient wrong. She arrives just in time to be swapped magically with the dying marchioness of Roxbury, and as a result the very American Miss Cunningham winds up married to the duke of Wessex, an English spymaster who has been ordered by the king to wed before he goes on his next mission. Soon the newlyweds find themselves caught up in plots and intrigues that lead them to France and a discovery of earth-shattering proportions.

52. Paulsen, Gary. *The Transall Saga.* Delacourte Press, 1998. **M J**
Thirteen-year-old Mark is off on his own, backpacking across the old Magruder Missile Range in the desert. A tube of blue-white light appears, and, when Mark goes to investigate, a rattler lunges at him, knocking him off the rock and into the brilliant beam of light. Mark is out cold. When he awakens, he finds himself on a strange planet, a world of red grass and trees, unrecognizable plant and animal life, and initially, no human beings. Thus begins Paulsen's most unusual survival story, one set in a different universe. Mark must find food, shelter, and, eventually, people—to help him return to his normal life on Earth.

53. Pullman, Philip. *His Dark Materials: The Golden Compass.* Alfred A. Knopf, 1996. **M J S**
In a sweeping fantasy saga of epic proportions, Pullman has created new universes bursting with heroic characters and malevolent evil. Heroine Lyra Belacqua and her daemon, Pantalaimon, inhabit the university world of Jordan College. Lyra becomes the guardian of a mysterious device called the Golden Compass, though she is initially unaware of its powers. Rumors fill the air that someone is kidnapping children and severing them from their soul-like companions, daemons. There also is the puzzling interest in Dust, a phenomenon that is somehow linked to the existence of other worlds. Lyra sets out to solve these horrible mysteries, befriended by a fierce armored bear

and aided by angels and witches. Complex and thrilling, this modern classic is a heart-pounding fantasy that is more violent than its American dust jacket artwork indicates. Sequels: *The Subtle Knife*; *The Amber Spyglass*.

54. Shetterly, Will. *Elsewhere*. Harcourt, 1991. **J S**
Bordertown is a strange mix of magic and technology, a place between the real world and the world of faerie that is filled with runaways, elves, halfies, and gangs. Teenager Ron Starbuck enters this cyberpunk world looking for his brother, Tony. Once a member of this bizarre community, Ron must come to terms with his own fears and alienation. Murky and quirky. Sequel: *Nevernever*.

55. Turtledove, Harry. *Worldwar: In the Balance. The Alternate History of Alien Invasion*. Ballantine Books, 1993. **J S**
It is 1942 and the world is at war. Germany, Russia, France, China, Japan, England, and the United States are all involved in the struggle when the real enemy arrives. Fleetlord Atvar and his lizard-like race have come to conquer Earth, which they call Tosev 3. Probes have shown them what kind of resistance to expect, so they are prepared for mounted knights in full armor. Instead, the lizards face guns and planes and tanks and General Patton as well as a bitter winter that stops them in their tracks. This is the first in a series in which the lizards and the big uglies (humans) battle for the fate of the Earth. Sequels: *Worldwar: Tilting the Balance*; *Worldwar: Upsetting the Balance*; *Worldwar: Striking the Balance*.

56. Wilson, Robert Charles. *Mysterium*. Bantam Books, 1994. **J S**
The government is conducting tests on a strange piece of radioactive jade that was unearthed at an archaeological dig in Turkey. One night there is a flash of blinding light at a secret research facility near a small town in Michigan. Afterward, the facility and town literally disappear from the face of Earth and reappear on another world that is in the middle of a war of religious intolerance. When military forces from this world invade the town from Earth, the inhabitants discover that they are regarded as heretics and that there is a plan to drop a nuclear bomb on them. The only hope for the people from Earth is to break into the research facility and try to escape by reactivating whatever caused them to be transported to this world in the first place.

57. Zelazny, Roger. *A Dark Traveling*. Walker and Company, 1987. **M J**
Fourteen-year-old James Wiley lives in a world in which the forces of

evil and good inhabit alternate universes, or bands. Lightbands are the home of normal human endeavors, and the enemy live in darkbands. There are also deadbands, either destroyed accidentally by technology that has been used incorrectly or deliberately sabotaged by darkband infiltrators. When his father disappears, James calls on his adopted sister, the witch Becky, for help. Joined by Barry, a trained assassin and karate expert, the three use magic to teleport to alternate worlds in their search for the missing scientist. There is one further complication because James has reached puberty. Since he takes after his uncle, he is in the process of becoming a werewolf. Ultimately, these three young people must confront an evil sorcerer to save the day in this delightful farce.

Biotechnology

Dolly exists, the human genome has been mapped; what next? In these futuristic stories, the human being is genetically enhanced—the question asked, is this good for civilization?

58. Ames, Mildred. *Anna to the Infinite Power*. Scribners, 1981. **M J**
    Twelve-year-old Anna is a real gem: a genius at mathematics, a budding kleptomaniac, and a potential sociopath with no feelings or concern for anyone else except herself. Then brother Rowan, two years her senior, takes his little sister to an intelligence-amplifier exhibit at the museum, where they meet an exact double of Anna. Confronting their mother, they learn that Anna is part of a classified government program, one of a number of clones of the brilliant physicist Anna Zimmerman who died working on a replicator breakthrough. Just when Anna is beginning to change and develop some empathy for those around her, the government takes her away for testing. Actually Anna soon discovers that she and the other clones are considered part of a failed project and are scheduled for destruction. Fortunately for her, Rowan's newly developed feelings of responsibility for his sister spur him on to try to visit and then to rescue her.

59. Brin, David. *Glory Season*. Bantam Books, 1993. **S**
    Maia and Leie are twins, not cossetted winterling clones but summerling vars, or variants, with an actual father. Instead of prized household daughters, they are merely extra mouths to feed until they come of age and can be sent out into the world. At age fifteen, the twins set sail together but are attacked by pirates and separated. For the first time, Maia is completely on her own and begins taking responsibility for her

own life. Maia also stumbles across a plot to make males active out of season, which could destroy her clone-dominated society if it is brought to fruition. Maia's efforts to foil this plot lead to incredible discoveries about her world and her place in it.

60. Crichton, Michael. *Jurassic Park*. Alfred A. Knopf, 1990. **J S**
A technique has been discovered that makes it possible for scientists to recover DNA from dinosaur bones and actually clone living, breathing dinosaurs. When an entrepreneur tries to build a dinosaur theme park, he discovers that it is almost impossible to protect yourself from dinosaurs run amok. Sequel: *The Lost World*.

61. Lasky, Kathryn. *Star Split*. Hyperion, 1999. **M J**
Daria lives in a future world in which genetically enhanced humans, genhants, are the norm. Daria herself is one of these creations; disease and other negative genetic matter have simply been eliminated from life on Earth, although the Bio Union does forbid vanity enhancements as unworthy endeavors. Daria finds that she is attracted to The Originals, people who have had no genetic changes made to their bodies. The reason for her curiosity about these people doesn't surface until Daria discovers on a mountain-climbing trip that she is actually a clone: another forbidden choice called umbellation that people secretly chose to save their unique genetic code and thereby live forever. Lasky adds a wealth of detail about the scientific process of cloning, a topic much in the news. It's when Daria discovers her parents' actions and they all face extinction that this science fiction novel takes off into the fantastic.

62. McCaffrey, Anne. *The Ship Who Sang*. Ballantine Books, 1976. **J S**
Severely deformed at birth, Helva nevertheless had other qualities that qualified her for entrance into the Brainship program. At the completion of her training, her body was placed in the titanium column of a spaceship and she became its brains. As a shellperson, Helva served as the heart and soul of the ship, but for legs she needed a softperson, or brawn, as her pilot. Once Helva selected a compatible brawn, she could begin working to pay back the debt she owed the government. This collection of connected stories describes Helva's efforts to find a brawn she could live with that could also survive missions that grew steadily more dangerous. When Helva finally does find the right brawn, her song of joy is unforgettable. Sequels: *Partnership* (with Margaret Ball); *The Ship Who Searched* (with Mercedes Lackey); *The City Who*

Fought (with S. M. Stirling); *The Ship Who Won* (with Jody Lynn Nye); *The Ship Errant* (with Jody Lynn Nye); *The Ship Avenged* (with S. M. Stirling).

63. Ore, Rebecca. *Gaia's Toys*. TOR Books, 1995. **S**
In the tradition of *Neuromancer* (see no. 141), the future is a dark, bleak place with the government in charge of welfare rolls filled with drode heads. Overpopulation has become an asset now that humans can have biocomponents surgically implanted that enable them to be plugged into a computer. After all, it's cheaper to make a computer that can read brain output than to build an effective artificial intelligence system. Willie is one of these drode heads, a combat veteran who now lives on the dole and fights his wars in cyberspace. Allison, a former member of an ecoterrorist group that detonated a bomb in New Orleans, is working for the feds. Together they are trying to find the scientist who created new genetic-modified insects such as the mantis that puts out tranquilizing pheromones or the wasps that sting when exposed to angry emotions. These are the toys that Gaia, the Earth, needs to take back control from her worst enemy—humankind.

64. Young, Jim. *Armed Memory*. TOR Books, 1995. **S**
Thanks to businesses such as Microde City, it is now possible to change genetic codes at will. Tim Wandel comes to the Big Apple looking for a job and finds one working on genetic codes for his cousin, Johnny Stevens, the biotech wizard who owns Microde City. Soon Tim is involved in Johnny's battle against a bloodthirsty society of hammerheads, victims of a virus that has made them physically more shark-like and placed them mentally under the control of the great ones. The hammerheads' goal is to destroy all two- and four-legged life-forms, in essence to purge the Earth of dryland dwellers and return control to the masters of the deep. Only a retromicrode virus, developed by Microde City, can stop this attack. But if the retromicrode virus is implemented, humankind will never be the same.

Brain Power

Characters in these novels have powers that humans often dream of: telekinetic abilities, empathic understanding, soul-bonding. Teens such as Davy in *Jumper* can escape the violence and evil in their world, simply by transporting themselves elsewhere.

65. Asaro, Catherine. *Primary Inversion*. TOR Books, 1994. **S**
Sauscony Valdoria, potential heir to the Skolian empire, is a bioengineered fighter pilot and elite officer in the space command. A primary, she's the leader of a four-person team that has landed on the planet Delos for well-earned rest and relaxation, a planet that steadfastly maintains its neutrality in the war between the Skolians and the caste-bound Traders. On this visit to Delos, Sauscony meets the heir to the Trader empire and discovers that instead of sadistically preying on the lower classes like the other Trader elite, he is an empath like she is. In fact, he may be the soul mate she never thought she would find. Or he could be her deadliest enemy. Sequel: *The Radiant Seas*.

66. Gould, Steven C. *Jumper*. TOR Books, 1992. **S**
When Davy is about to be beaten by his drunken father, he discovers that he is a jumper and teleports to a place of safety—the fiction section of his public library. When he tries to run away and accepts a ride from the wrong trucker, he is saved from a brutal rape by teleporting again—back to the library. His next attempt at flight is successful, and he makes it all the way to New York City. There he discovers that a sixteen-year-old with no birth certificate, driver's license, social security number, or parental consent form can't make an honest living, so he uses his newfound talent to rob a bank. He also meets and falls in

love with a college student, makes Arab terrorists his new cause, and slips through the fingers of the special agents the government sends after him.

67. Greeno, Gayle. *The Ghatti's Tale: Book One: Finders-Seekers*. Daw Books, 1993. **S**
The catlike ghatti bond telepathically with a soul mate and accompany these seekers as they travel their assigned circuit, listening to complaints, ferreting out the truth, and pronouncing judgment. Now something is seriously wrong in Methuen. Seekers and their ghatti are disappearing or are found dead, their bodies twisted and torn and their brains scooped out. Doyce and her bond mate, Khar'pern, are devastated when her fiance is one of these victims and his ghat, Saam, has no memory of what happened, his mind stripped clean and his ability to mindspeak gone. While backtracking Oriel's last circuit, Doyce and Khar'pern stumble upon a plot that could spell doom for all of the ghatti and seekers on Methuen. Sequels: *Mind-Speakers' Call*; *Exile's Return*.

68. Henderson, Zenna. *Pilgrimage: The Book of the People*. Gollancz, 1962. **J S**
The People are aliens who look like humans but have very special mental abilities, and the stories in this collection show just how much danger they would be in if humans discovered their secret. The People are united by religious beliefs and societal customs, but it is their gifts of telekinesis, teleportation, and mental telepathy that set them apart. The People isolate themselves as much as possible from true humans, but at the same time, they are ever vigilant, listening for the cry for help from any of their members on the outside trying to come home to a safe haven. Sequel: *The People: No Different Flesh*.

69. Lackey, Mercedes. *Brightly Burning*. Daw Books, 2000. **J S**
The author returns to Valdemar with its feudal society and mysterious horse-like companions who select as bond mates candidates for herald training. The protagonist, young Lavan, has recently moved to Haven. His parents are respected members of the guilds, and Lavan hates the thought of following in their capable footsteps. That's why he is delighted to be offered a reprieve, an opportunity to go to a school established by the trade guilds where he will have a chance to study and eventually select the guild that appeals to him the most. At school, Lavan is the victim of vicious bullies preying on the younger students; he

discovers to his shock that he can fight back. Anger and a sense of injustice release his powerful talent, that of a firestarter. However, uncontrolled, his talent threatens his life and that of those around him until a companion claims him and he enters the Colegium to train as a herald. So begins the training of Lavan Firestarter, who later goes to war to protect his land from invasion. Prequels: *The Last Herald Mage: Magic's Pawn*; *Magic's Promise*; *Magic's Price*.

70. Lackey, Mercedes. *Winds of Fury*. Daw Books, 1993. **S**
In this concluding volume of The Winds Trilogy, Valdemar is under attack by the evil Mornelithe and the forces of the mysterious eastern empire. Elspeth, a herald and heir to the throne of Valdemar, has come to the vale of the taledras for training as an adept. While there she helps heal the heartstone in the vale and befriends a family of gryphons. Vanyel, the last herald-mage, makes a surprise appearance to show his descendants why magic had to be kept out of Valdemar until now and what steps they needed to save their home in this final struggle against the forces of evil. Prequels: *Winds of Fate*; *Winds of Change*.

71. McCaffrey, Anne. *Pegasus in Flight*. Ballantine Books, 1990. **J S**
In an overcrowded, overpolluted future in which birth control is strictly regulated, talents such as extrasensory perception and telekinetic abilities have become extremely valuable. Rhyssa Owen, director of the Jerhattan Parapsychic Center, protects the talents in her care while constantly looking for new wild talents to bring into her center. Her latest finds include Peter, a boy with a severed spine able to tap into electric energy and move anything, including himself in out-of-body sessions, and twelve-year-old Tirla, an instantaneous translator with the ability to calm and soothe in a dozen or more languages. Tirla's birth was illegal. Consequently she has been hiding in the mall not only from government forces but also from sick individuals who prey on helpless children. Tirla is far from helpless, however, as those who try to hurt her soon discover. Prequel: *To Ride Pegasus*. Sequels: *The Rowan*; *Damia*; *Damia's Children*; *Lyon's Pride*; *The Tower and the Hive*.

72. Resnick, Mike. *Soothsayer*. Ace, 1991. **S**
Eight-year-old Penelope Bailey is the soothsayer. She can foresee all possible futures and then manipulate current events so that the future she likes best is the one that comes true. Mouse is a thief who discovers Penelope in chains, rescues her from her alien captor, and becomes a surrogate mother to her. Now the two are on the run, chased by

bounty hunters and government agents. Penelope is dangerous enough as a child (her gift is still relatively weak); what will happen if she is allowed to grow up? Can an angry adult Penelope destroy entire worlds, as the child has destroyed the bounty hunters? Sequels: *Oracle*; *Prophet*.

73. Tolan, Stephanie S. *Welcome to the Ark*. William Morrow, 1996. **M J**
The ark is the global family group home project, funded by the Laurel Mountain Center for Research and Rehabilitation Board. Doctors work at this facility with a small group of brilliant but mentally unstable children. The children include a phenom who claims she's an alien, an empath who shuts down after experiencing his mother's death, a computer whiz who has already attempted suicide once, and a young spiritualist who has been driven to schizophrenia. These children are successful in reaching out to others who are gifted until a doctor almost destroys them by using drugs to break the connection.

74. Van Vogt, A. E. *Slan*. Amereon, 1980. **J S**
This science fiction novel is a classic tale of alienation, isolation, and a life and death struggle for survival. Slan was different from those around him but managed to hide his special mental abilities from normal humans for years. When the government discovered his secret, Slan had no choice but to go on the run, pursued by frightened normal humans afraid of what he could do.

75. Vinge, Joan. *Psion*. Dell, 1990. **S**
Psion is an orphan captured by a government agency that specializes in training those gifted with latent mental abilities. The unknown opponent the orphan is trained to fight is powerful enough to take over the civilized world and would have succeeded, except for the unexpected resistance he met in Psion. Sequels: *Catspaw*; *Dreamfall*.

Brave New Worlds

Whether it's creating a new environment on an existing planet such as Mars or establishing in the reader's mind the world of Darkover, these stories capture the imagination with their "what if's" of planetary history.

76. Bear, Greg. *Moving Mars*. St. Martin's Press, 1993. **S**
When Casseia joined a college student movement protesting the closing of her university on Mars, she never dreamed that it would lead to a life in politics. It was during her presidency that war between Earth and Mars became inevitable. The outcome was never in doubt, considering the state of nanotechnology on Earth, but then the scientists on Mars discovered a way actually to move the planet beyond Earth's sphere of influence.

77. Bova, Ben. *Mars*. Bantam Books, 1992. **S**
The first expedition to search for life on the planet Mars becomes embroiled in political infighting because of the actions of geologist Jamie Waterman, of mixed white and Navaho heritage. He is so moved upon first stepping out on the surface of the planet that he utters a Navaho expression. Since mission control cannot interpret this phrase, the media, the vice president, and the authorities become convinced that Jamie is some kind of Native American activist. As a result, the scientific discoveries that the members of the expedition make are overshadowed by what is taking place within the political community back on Earth. Sequel: *Return to Mars*.

78. Bradley, Marion Zimmer. *Exile's Song*. Daw Books, 1996. **J S**
Margaret Alton, daughter of the Darkovan representative to the Terran

Imperial Senate, was whisked away from the planet as a very young child. Now a young woman and with no knowledge of her heritage, Margaret has returned to Darkover with a college professor collecting folk songs. After he dies of a heart attack, the headaches and visions that have always troubled Margaret get stronger, leading to an attack of threshold illness that almost kills her. This is caused by her rapidly developing laran, or mental abilities. During her recovery, she discovers that she is an heiress on Darkover with family obligations that involve political alliances and an arranged marriage. The fact that Margaret has plans of her own means nothing to her new relatives until she uses her newly awakened laran to remind them that she has a mind of her own. Prequels: *The Heritage of Hastur*; *Sharra's Exile*. Sequels: *The Shadow Matrix*; *The Traitor's Sun*.

79. Bradley, Marion Zimmer. *Hawkmistress*! Daw Books, 1982. **J S**
Because she is just a girl, Romilly's father refuses to believe that she has the MacAran gift, the ability to communicate with animals. When he tries to force her into an arranged marriage with a lecherous neighbor, the young girl runs away. Romilly's country is involved in a civil war, and she soon finds a position tending Sentry Birds for the king. She is also accepted as a swordswoman among the Free Amazons, but then her magical laran begins to stir. This marks the blossoming of mental powers so strong that only the magicians in the towers can save her—provided Romilly gets to them before it is too late.

80. Bradley, Marion Zimmer and Mercedes Lackey. *Rediscovery: A Novel of Darkover*. Daw Books, 1994. **S**
Terrans landing on the planet Darkover uncover the remains of the lost colony ship, proof positive that this strange, dark planet was first settled by humans from Earth. When the crew is able to communicate with the natives using rudimentary telepathic powers, a bond develops that is shattered when the visitors use firearms to settle a dispute.

81. Brunner, John. *A Maze of Stars*. Ballantine, 1991. **S**
The sentient *Ship* travels the Arm of Stars, first seeding barren planets with human life and then returning over a period of thousands of years, checking on human progress and development. Occasionally, *Ship* takes on passengers, but its preset task and schedule prevent it from becoming too involved with the diverse worlds of the universe. More a collection of short stories within a framework than a true novel, Brun-

ner's tale still holds the reader with its changing cast of characters, its sweeping, panoramic perspective, and the gradually emerging presence of *Ship* itself.

82. Hoover, H. M. *The Winds of Mars*. Dutton, 1995. **J S**
Seventeen-year-old Annalyn Reynolds Court is the legal daughter of the president of Mars. Her mother, commander of a star-probe vessel, left Mars orbit a few months after Annalyn's birth. The girl was raised in the wing of Fountain House, the sanctuary where the members of the president's new family live. She likes her stepbrother, Evan, but his mother, Janis, is a beautiful tyrant. When Annalyn and Evan grow up, they are sent to the military academy where Annalyn receives a gift from her mother—her very own personal security robot named Hector Protector. Hector has been programmed to save Annalyn's life and does so in the rebellion that reveals the truth about her father.

83 Kagan, Janet. *Mirabile*. TOR, 1991. **J S**
Mirabile is a planet where genetic mutations, known as dragon's teeth, keep popping up. The friendly mutants are kept as part of the gene pool, but the deadly or dangerous ones have to be sought out and destroyed. Deciding which is which is the job of Annie Jason Masmajean and her gene readers. Their humorous adventures are related in six connected stories that include encounters with creatures such as the Loch Moose Monster, the Kangaroo Rex, and Frankenswine.

84. LeGuin, Ursula K. *The Left Hand of Darkness*. Ace Books, 1971. **J S**
Genly Ai, ambassador to the planet Winter, goes from pampered guest to fugitive, escaping across the frozen wastes accompanied by his mentor, a former leader of the planet also fleeing for his life. During the course of their trek, the ambassador makes an amazing discovery. This is a culture where the inhabitants regularly alternate between the masculine and feminine genders, a fact that causes him to look at his mentor in an entirely new light.

85. McCaffrey, Anne and Jody Lynn Nye. *Decision at Doona*. Ballantine, 1975. **S**
When humans first landed on Doona, they thought they were the only sentient species on the planet. Discovering that the catlike Hrrubans were already on the planet should have meant the departure of the humans, but because of the friendship between two young boys, the human Todd Reeve and the Hrruban Hrriss, a treaty was

established between these sentient species that enabled both groups to share the planet. Sequels: *Crisis on Doona*; *Treaty at Doona*.

86. McCaffrey, Anne and Elizabeth Ann Scarborough. *Powers That Be*. Del Ray, 1993. **S**
Major Yanaba Maddock, retired from the service because her lungs were injured in a poison gas attack, has been sent to the planet Petaybe by Intergal. Her mission is to search for missing scientific and survey teams and try to discover why mineral deposits that show up on long-range scans can never be located by observers on the ground. As her investigation deepens, Yanaba finds that the planet itself is a sentient being, helping both animals and people live in an almost symbiotic relationship as they struggle against their common enemy: the bitter cold and the outsiders bent on exploiting the planet's resources. Instead of reporting her findings to Intergal, the major finds herself joining the struggle on the side of the planet. Sequels: *Power Lines*; *Power Play*.

87. Pohl, Frederik and C. M. Kornbluth. *The Space Merchants*. Ballantine, 1953. **J S**
Written in the 1950s, this is a prophetic look at what advertising has become over the past fifty years. It is a work of fiction, so no one believed at the time it was written that a company would actually make people addicted to its product to increase sales, as the tobacco companies have been discovered to do today. This humorous novel is a perfect warning of what is in store if the marketing people ever gain total control of society. Sequel: *Merchant's War* (by Frederik Pohl).

88. Robinson, Kim Stanley. *Red Mars*. Bantam Books, 1992. **S**
The first of a trilogy, this Hugo award-winning novel describes in impressive detail the establishment of a settlement on the planet Mars. Conflict arises when two new societies are formed: the Reds, who want to leave the planet alone, and the Greens, who are proponents of change and hydroplaning. The future of the planet and the people living on it will ultimately depend on which group is the victor in this struggle. Sequels: *Green Mars*; *Blue Mars*.

89. Sheffield, Charles. *Summertide*. Ballantine Books, 1990. **J S**
Book One of the Heritage Universe describes what happens on the planet Quake during summertide. At that time, there is a Grand Conjunction of the stars and planets in the entire system, which only occurs every 350,000 years. A group of foolhardy visitors insists on braving the surface of the planet as the Conjunction approaches, but instead of

getting a better look at this event, they discover that there are some things it is better to experience from afar. Sequels: *Divergence: The Heritage Universe, Book 2*; *Transcendence: The Heritage Universe, Book 3*.

90. Vinge, Joan. *The Snow Queen*. Doubleday, 1980. **S**
Arienrhod has been the queen of winter on the planet Tiamat for the past 150 years—with the help of an elixir of life distilled from slaughtered sea mer. Now summer is coming to the planet, and when it arrives, Arienrhod and her consort Starbuck are to be drowned to make way for the summer queen. The snow queen, however, has made other plans. Instead of dying at her appointed time, Arienrhod plans to sacrifice her potential replacement, the clone Moon, sent to grow up among the summer people but expected back in time for the ceremony. Sequels: *World's End*; *The Summer Queen*. Prequel: *Tangled Up in Blue*.

91. Wolfe, Gene. *On Blue's Waters. The First Volume of The Book of the Short Sun*. TOR Books, 1999. **S**
The protagonist, Horn, now a papermaker living on Blue, was the narrator who described the adventures of Patera Silk in a previous series, *The Book of the Long Sun*. Now Horn has adventures of his own as he goes on a quest, his mission to return to the Whorl and bring Patera Silk to Blue, which is in need of a strong, honest calde. Prequels: *The Book of the New Sun: The Shadow of the Torturer*; *The Claw of the Conciliator*; *The Sword of the Torturer*; *The Citadel of the Conciliator*. *The Book of the Long Sun: Nightside the Long Sun*; *Lake of the Long Sun*; *Calde of the Long Sun*; *Exodus from the Long Sun*. Sequel: *In Green's Jungles*.

Double, Double, Toil and Trouble

Witches and wizards, cauldrons and sorcerers: there's always been a wealth of magical stories for fantasy readers, long before the appearance of the Harry Potter phenomenon.

92. Anthony, Piers. *A Spell for Chameleon*. Random House, 1997. **M J S**
    Magic rules in this enchanted land. In fact, every citizen in Xanth has a special spell except for poor Bink. Bink lived in a world of centaurs, dragons, and basilisks, but despite the fact that Good Magician Humfrey and Beauregard the Genie believe that Bink possesses quite powerful magic, no one else does. Unless he is able to prove his powers, he will be exiled to Mundania, where the Evil Magician Trent is waiting for him. Sequels include: *The Source of Magic*; *Castle Roogna*; *Centaur Aisle*; *Ogre, Ogre*; *Night Mare*; *Dragon on a Pedestal*; *Crewel Lye*; *A Caustic Yarn*; *Golem in the Gears*.

93. Bradley, Marion Zimmer, Julian May, and Andre Norton. *Lady of the Trillium*. Bantam Books, 1995. **J S**
    This sequel to the Trillium trilogy takes place several hundred years after three sisters reunited the Trillium petals and saved their world. When the novel opens, Haramis, the eldest sister and a powerful sorcerer, is the guardian under whose protection the land of Ruwenda has prospered. Now it is time for her to start preparing her successor, and she begins her search with water-scrying. When Haramis sees two royal children, a boy and a girl, she naturally selects the twelve-year-old girl Mikayla to follow in her footsteps. In her efforts to separate the two, she chooses to ignore that Mikayla and Fiolon have been inseparable since they were seven, they are already pledged to one another,

and incredible as it seems, Fiolon also has magical abilities. Hardest of all to overcome is the fact that Mikayla is every bit as stubborn and strong willed as Haramis. Prequels: *Black Trillium*; *Golden Trillium*; *Blood Trillium*.

94. Charnas, Suzy McKee. *The Bronze King*. Houghton Mifflin, 1985. **M J**
    This is a delightful fantasy in the urban fairie tradition. Set in New York City, it is an exciting account of how one young girl, a spoiled musical prodigy, and a bronze king cum homeless person are able to save the world from the Kraken. Fourteen-year-old Valentine is going home from school one day when she hears an explosion and is struck above the eye by something. As a result, she becomes the focal point for a magical battle that is causing things to disappear. The urbanization of society has weakened the wards guarding the Kraken, and now he is free. The Kraken's first attack causes the statue of the bronze king in Central Park to disappear. Val meets an old fiddler named Paevo and a young musician named Joel, and together they set out to save the world, assisted by Val's senile Granny Gran who is in a nursing home but still has some connections to Sorcery Hall. Against them are the Kraken's three dark princes as street gang members and Val's mother, who doesn't understand why her daughter's grades are slipping and why she's hanging out with an old man. Consequently, Val is grounded before the final battle. But Joel has been captured by the Kraken, and nothing is going to keep Val from rescuing him.

95. Duane, Diane. *So You Want to be a Wizard*. Harcourt Brace, 1996. **M**
    Nita finds a library book that gives instructions on how to become a wizard. When she meets Kit, another kid wizard, they search for a book that will help them solve cosmic problems. Duane's series moves undersea in the second volume, *Deep Wizardry*, and then into the cyberworld in *High Wizardry*. In book four, *A Wizard Abroad*, Nita and Kit, now teens, make a time travel jump to an alternative Manhattan to escape bullies.

96. Goodkind, Terry. *Wizard's First Rule*. TOR Books, 1994. **S**
    Richard's father was murdered and his older brother, Michael, is more interested in politics than in spending time with him. Fortunately, the old man Zedd who practically raised him is still there for Richard. While investigating his father's death, Richard saves the life of a woman in a white dress from the Quad, four warrior assassins. She is Kahlan, Mother Confessor and last survivor in the Midlands. Kahlan

has crossed the boundary and entered the Westlands looking for the old Wizard and the Seeker of Truth, who turn out to be Zedd and Richard. Both Richard and Kahlan have secrets. His is the fact that he has committed *The Book of Counted Sorrows* to memory, including information about the boxes being sought by the evil Darken Rahl. Hers is mind control and the ability to kill with the touch of love, which means their growing passion for each other must remain purely platonic . . . at least at first. Sequels: *Stone of Tears*; *Blood of the Fold*; *Temple of the Winds*; *Soul of the Fire*; *Sword of Truth*; *Faith of the Fallen*.

97. Hambly, Barbara. *Stranger at the Wedding*. Ballantine, 1994. **S**
Kyra is a journeyman wizard preparing for her final test at the Citadel of Wizards when everything starts to go wrong. She begins having ominous dreams, her spells stop working the way they are supposed to, and the skrying water she looks into turns to blood. That's when she realizes that she is seeing her younger sister, Alix, dead on her wedding night. If Kyra wants to save her sister's life, she must interrupt her studies and return to the real world. This means returning to the home of her father, a wealthy merchant who rejected her six years ago when she turned to a life of magic. To Kyra's surprise, her father allows her to stay for her sister's wedding but treats her with considerable scorn. Then Kyra meets her sister's intended, Spens, the mayor's son. She is unimpressed with this silent, brooding, ill-dressed bear of a man, proof positive that first impressions can be deceiving. Kyra certainly has her work cut out for her. She must stop the wedding, at least temporarily, without letting the Inquisition discover she is using magic; find and deactivate the death spell placed on Alix; discover who is behind this threat and why; and, above all, control her own rebellious heart when she realizes she is falling in love with her sister's fiance.

98. Ibbotson, Eva. *Which Witch?* Penguin Putnam, 1999. **M**
Arriman the Awful, wizard extraordinaire, is in a snit because his replacement hasn't shown up; he wishes to retire. Solution: Marry a very powerful witch, beget an heir, and retire in style and comfort. Having no romantic appeal, Arriman has no takers for his matrimonial plans. What to do? Hold a contest, of course, and the winner, who will obviously be a witch of immense black power, will certainly produce the most capable offspring. Full of tongue-in-cheek humor, Ibbotson's story is played strictly for laughs, skewering every element of traditional witch tales.

99. Jones, Diana Wynne. *Charmed Life*. William Morrow, 1998. **M**
Orphans Cat Chant and his sister, Gwendolyn, land at Chrestomanci
the Enchanter's castle, learning the essential spells in witchcraft, not
always to the master wizard's plan. Jones continues in *The Magicians
of Caprona*; *Witch Week*; and *The Lives of Christopher Chant*.

100. Jones, Diana Wynne. *Dark Lord of Derkholm*. Greenwillow, 1998. **M
J S**
This marvelous fantasy is set in a world full of wizards, battles, magical beasts, demons, and worst of all, an avaricious human business-
man who has run roughshod over its inhabitants. Mr. Chesney has an
iron-clad contract for the annual pilgrim parties that he brings to
Derkholm and doesn't care that these tourists are practically de-
stroying the fantasy world. Wizard Derk, chosen as this year's Dark
Lord, and his son, Blade, have been foretold as the ones who will be
instrumental in abolishing the pilgrim parties and getting rid of Mr.
Chesney for good. Derk's specialty is not fighting but growing things
and breeding special creatures such as griffins, winged horses, and
flying pigs. So Derk ineptly raises a blue demon, is fried by a dragon,
and watches in despair as his world is laid waste again by the passage of the pilgrims and the battles staged for them between the
forces of good and evil—until he comes up with a plan that just
might succeed in changing everything. Sequel: *The Year of the Griffin*.

101. Jones, Diana Wynne. *A Sudden Wild Magic*. W. Morrow, 1992. **J S**
Witchcraft is alive and well in Britain, aided by the inner circle led by
Agnes, who may be old but is definitely still with it. Agnes is the one
Mark Lister comes to with an important discovery. It seems another
universe has not only been spying on the Earth but also using it for research purposes. Global warming, AIDS, even the Chernobyl incident
were all instigated by Arth, which watches how humans cope with
these problems and then steals their solutions. The inner circle decides to send a commando mission to spread a plague virus on Arth.
At the last minute, Zillah and her two-year-old son, Marcus, join the
mission, which then ends disastrously, with the plague virus destroyed and three-quarters of the ship's passengers dead. However,
the six surviving women still have something up their sleeves to attack Arth with. Jones blends magical battles, centaurs, mental manipulation, romance, child care, and gallivanting through the galaxies in
this complex novel.

102. Jones, Diana Wynne. *Howl's Moving Castle*. Greenwillow, 1986. **M J S**
Sophie is the oldest of three sisters, and in true fairy tale fashion, she knows that nothing wonderful will ever happen to her. Sure enough, when the wicked Witch of the Waste comes into her hat shop and doesn't like the selection available there, it is Sophie who suffers, turned into an old woman by the witch. Not knowing what to do, Sophie hobbles out of town and gets a job working for Wizard Howl in his Moving Castle. There she befriends a blue fire demon, copes with Howl's inept assistant, finds herself pursued by a living scarecrow, adopts a mangy dog, and is inevitably drawn into Howl's plans. The wizard is vainly seeking spells to protect himself against the wiles of the Witch of the Waste. An inveterate womanizer, to Sophie's horror Howl also seems to be at the point of making a conquest of her own sister! All's well that ends well, though, in this gentle fairy tale spoof full of humor and sparkling dialogue. Heroine Sophie learns that there can be something magical in being the oldest sister after all. Sequel: *Castle in the Air*.

103. Lee, Tanith. *Black Unicorn*. Simon & Schuster, 1989. **M J**
The sorceress Jaive and her unmagical daughter, Tanaquil, live in a desert fortress. Tanaquil is supremely bored with her isolated life and at sixteen begins to wonder about her father. One day, out messing about in the dreary and barren landscape, Tanaquil's pet, Peeve, finds some extraordinary bones. Tanaquil brings the bones back to the castle, puts them together, and hangs them as a mobile in her room. They form a magical creature, a unicorn. In a fit, Jaive inadvertently sends some magic dust over the skeleton, and the unicorn comes to life, flying out of the castle and across the desert. Tanaquil follows, finally setting off on her search for her real father and determined to deal with the magical creature brought to life through her mother's powers. Sequels: *Gold Unicorn*; *Red Unicorn*.

104. Norton, Andre. *Songsmith: A Witch World Novel*. TOR Books, 1992. **J S**
Lady Eydrth from the land of Arvon, Kar Garuduryn, is a songsmith of the greatest talent. She leaves her homeland and castle to rescue her father, Jervon, and mother, Elys, both of whom have been ensorcelled by powerful magic. Eydrth first seeks the advice of the witches in Es. Rebuffed by the sorceresses, she finds help from the young apprentice, Avris. Avris and Eydrth change places so that Avris can escape her forced apprenticeship, and Avris, magically disguised as Eydrth, leaves castle Es and Eydrth follows. After Avris is returned to her

beloved Logor in Kastryn, the songsmith sets out for the city of Lomt and the wisdom of the healing scrolls—documents that might aid her in finding a cure for her father's mind sickness. During her journey, Eydrth meets Kadar, or Alon, one of her own people. Together with the Keplian Monso—a horse-like creature—and a powerful falcon, they begin the long quest to heal Jervon and release Elys from a nine-year enchantment. Filled with adventure, teen characters, fantastical creatures, and an aura of menacing magic, this is one of Norton's most readable Witch World novels. (Norton has many novels and short story collections set in Witch World, and several series.)

105. Pierce, Tamora. *Sandry's Book. Circle of Magic. Book One.* Scholastic, 1997. **M J**
This is the first in a quartet that features four young people with very special talents but no clue of how to use them—at least at first. Sandry is the Lady Sandrilene fa Toren, a member of the nobility who discovers she can weave light into a skein of colorful threads when she is locked away in a small room. Sandry is rescued by Niklaren Goldeye, a mage who finds people with hidden talents. Second in the group is Daja, rescued from the southeastern Pebbled Sea after she was the sole survivor of a shipwreck. Because of her bad luck, Daja was cast out by the traders and so ends up at Winding Circle Temple and its school for mages. The third in the group is Briar, the only boy, a young thief who was caught and given the choice of going with Niklaren or a life of servitude at the docks. Fourth is Tris, a merchant's daughter kicked out of her previous school because of the destruction she leaves behind when she loses her temper. Together these four will learn how to use their magical abilities for the good of others, forming a circle of magic that is even stronger than what they can do as individuals. Sequels: *Tris's Book*; *Daja's Book*; *Briar's Book*.

106. Pratchett, Terry. *Faust/Eric.* Gollancz, 1990. **J S**
Fourteen-year-old Eric is trying to raise a demon when he makes a mistake and instead gets Rincewind, the most incompetent wizard in the universe, followed everywhere by his hostile, unstoppable walking luggage. Eric refuses to believe that Rincewind is not a demon and demands three wishes: the most beautiful woman who has ever lived, mastery of all the kingdoms of the world, and to live forever. In typical tongue-in-cheek style, Pratchett makes fun of all the fantasy conventions, beginning with the wishes. Eric becomes master of all the world of a primitive people who then plan to execute him. He appears to the

Fair Elenor Tsort, who like Helen of Troy, has caused a war. Unfortunately, the Fair Elenor has been a captive for years and years and has eaten a lot of pasta during that time. Finally, doesn't it count as living forever when you are there with the creator at the beginning of things and then wind up in Hell? This is just one of several adventures set on Discworld, the only flat earth in the universe, a world that is carried by four elephants riding on the back of a giant turtle. Other titles in the series include: *The Colour of Magic*; *The Light Fantastic*; *Equal Rites*; *Mort*; *Guards! Guards!*; *Pyramids*; *Witches Abroad*; *Moving Pictures*; *Reaper Man*; *Wyrd Sisters*; *Sourcery*; *The Fifth Elephant*.

107. Rowling, J. K. *Harry Potter and the Sorcerer's Stone*. Scholastic, 1998. **M J**
Harry Potter's parents were killed when he was an infant. Harry survived the magical attack, which left him with a lightning-shaped scar on his forehead and the blazing reputation throughout wizardom as the boy who lived. Harry had a miserable childhood living with his aunt and uncle and their spoiled son, the rotten little tyrant Dudley. The Dursleys are Muggles, afraid of anything to do with magic, so they tell Harry nothing about his parents and punish him when he does anything the least bit magical. That all changes when Harry turns eleven and discovers that he is enrolled at Hogwarts School of Witchcraft and Wizardry, a most exclusive boarding school. There Harry becomes a star at Quidditch (air hockey played on flying broom sticks), makes new friends and deadly enemies, and comes face to face with his parents' murderer. The sorcerer's stone is an alchemist's key in this fast-paced, humorous, gloriously inventive fantasy. Sequels: *Harry Potter and the Secret Chamber*; *Harry Potter and the Prisoner of Azkaban*; *Harry Potter and the Goblet of Fire*.

108. Somtow, S. P. *The Wizard's Apprentice*. Macmillan, 1993. **M J**
This latest Dragon Flight fantasy is a light-hearted romp built around the theme of magic. A bright young teen, a marvel on his skateboard but pretty klutzy otherwise, discovers that he has previously undetected talents. He becomes a wizard's apprentice with some very special challenges to face. As the son of a special-effects genius, he is at least used to what the more explosive aspects of magic look like. While working for the wizard, he accidentally sets a smog monster loose on the city and then has to face a special-effects dragon gone crazy. There's lots of humor and a touch of romance as he manages to save Los Angeles after all.

109. Stevermer, Caroline. *A College of Magics*. TOR Books, 1994. **J S**
Faris Nallaneen, the eighteen-year-old duchess of Galazon, has been
sent to Greenlaw College by her uncle. At Greenlaw, magic is taught,
and at the end of three years, if Faris has the gift, she will graduate an
accomplished witch. There's skullduggery afoot, however. Fortunately Faris's uncle has foisted a bodyguard on her, the handsome and
extremely capable Tyrian, and he helps Faris survive several attacks.
Then, in her third year, the college administration discovers just how
powerful she already is and sends her off to meet with the Warden of
the West. There Faris learns that she is actually the Warden of the
North, come again after many years to heal the rift caused by the previous Warden, an exercise so dangerous that it may cost her her life.

110. Wrede, Patricia C. *Mairelon the Magician*. TOR Books, 1991. **J S**
Disguised as a boy, seventeen-year-old Kim has been hired to break
into the wagon of a traveling player to see if he has concealed a silver bowl there. The wagon actually belongs to a powerful wizard, and
Kim is captured in Mairelon the magician's protective spell. Instead
of turning her over to the Bow Street Runners, Mairelon enlists Kim's
help in trying to find the remaining pieces of the Saltash Set, a platter
and four crystal spheres that force the users to speak only the truth.
Mairelon, accused of having stolen the set some five years previously,
has been working undercover for the British government ever since.
He has recovered the bowl; now he's on the trail of the other pieces.
Mairelon takes Kim with him on his quest, begins teaching her magic
tricks, and discovers that she has a talent for real magic as well. The
quest becomes a comedy of errors as well as a mystery, which ends
with Mairelon making Kim his ward. Regency fans know where that
will lead! Sequel: *Magician's Ward*.

111. Zambreno, Mary Frances. *A Plague of Sorcerers*. Harcourt, 1991. **M**
Jermyn Graves doesn't think he can become a sorcerer—he doesn't
have a familiar and doesn't have the talent. Jermyn's Aunt Merovice
gets herself into a feud with the Weather Master Fulke. To help her,
Jermyn discovers that he does have a familiar, but it's not an ordinary
wizard's companion: it's Delia, his pet skunk! Finally apprenticed to
the Master Eschar, Jermyn is integral in solving court intrigues and a
decimating plague that threatens the kingdom. Multiple layers of
plots, a likable young teen, and that attractive skunk make this a perfect middle school read. Sequel: *Journeyman Wizard*.

Endangered Earth

Conserving Earth's resources, valuing clean air and water, disposing of toxic wastes: If humans consistently and devotedly cared for Earth, most of these novels would not have come to be.

112. Anderson, Kevin J. and Doug Beason. *Ill Wind: A Novel of Ecological Disaster*. St. Martin's Press, 1995. **J S**
After a massive oil spill in the San Francisco Bay, the oil company responsible authorizes the use of an experimental bacteria for the clean up. What no one knows is that the scientist who created this bacteria has a hidden agenda—he plans to use it to save the world from its dependence upon petroleum. The released bacteria does begin fighting the oil spill, but then it mutates and attacks everything made of plastic, eventually becoming a petroplague that spreads all over the world. With syringes beginning to disintegrate and airplanes literally dropping out of the sky, civilization as it has been known has come to an end. Humankind's only hope is the successful completion of a secret solar satellite project, but it will take an armed battle for this to happen.

113. Baird, Thomas. *Smart Rats*. HarperCollins, 1990. **J S**
Laddie Grayson is a seventeen-year-old trying to find a job—a next to impossible task in Earth's ecologically impoverished future. Although he tests in the top percentile intellectually, Laddie's parents refuse to send him to council school because it would call attention to his mother's poor health and the strange behavior of his sister. Laddie and his family are barely existing as rationed citizens, facing a gradual but steady decline in their quality of life. Then the

government announces a new progeny program designed to re-lieve Earth's population by reducing all families to just one child. The extra children must be sent away on government ships, and Laddie is chosen by his parents to join this program, leaving his antisocial sister at home. When Laddie discovers that the extra children are taken out to sea and drowned, he realizes that his survival depends upon something happening to his sister—the sooner the better.

114. Baxter, Stephen. *Moonseed*. HarperCollins, 1998. **S**
What if the moon rocks brought back from the first lunar expedition were more than just rocks? What if they were a form of moonseed, lying dormant until a few particles scattered on a lava crag in Scotland set off a chain reaction that will eventually lead to the destruction of the Earth? By the time scientists discover that the pool of dust caused by the moonseed will eventually consume the entire planet, it is too late to do anything but try to save as many people as possible by colonizing the moon. A large cast of characters faces an extinction event of unparalleled proportions in this fast-paced, end-of-the-world scenario, with the forces of science fighting a brave battle until the very end.

115. Bova, Ben with A. J. Austin. *To Save the Sun*. TOR Books, 1992. **S**
The sun is dying; when it is gone, Earth's distinctive gene pool will be destroyed as well. Humankind's only hope lies in the theories of a young scientist, but first she must convince the political and scientific communities that her theories will work. Once the decision has been made to put them to the test, she must go into cryosleep for a two-century wait. Then, upon being awakened, she will have an opportunity to apply her theories and take the necessary steps to rejuvenate the sun. Sequel: *To Fear the Light*.

116. Bradbury, Ray. *Fahrenheit 451*. Rupert Hart-Davis, 1954. **M J S**
Fahrenheit 451 is the temperature at which paper burns. The paper burned is in books, which are meticulously ferreted out and destroyed by firemen. The protagonist of Bradbury's tale is a fireman who begins to think about what he is doing for the very first time, an act that is both dangerous and perverted. As a result of these thoughts, he develops a new mission. He strives to become a walking book; his goal, to preserve messages from the past so that they will be available for future generations. A literate, beautifully writ-

ten, thought-provoking work that depicts book burning in an entirely different light.

117. Dickinson, Peter. *Eva*. Bantam, Doubleday, Dell, 1990. **J S**
When thirteen-year-old Eva's body is destroyed in a car wreck, her brain is transplanted into the body of a chimpanzee. This is not just any chimp. This animal is a member of the last group of chimps extant in a severely overpopulated world. Eva's father is the scientist working with this group of chimps, and she has grown up playing with them. Her remarkable adjustment to life in an animal's body and her struggle to bring about a greater degree of understanding and acceptance of the animals that share the planet make for intriguing reading indeed.

118. Farmer, Nancy. *The Ear, the Eye and the Arm*. Orchard, 1994. **M J S**
In Zimbabwe of 2194, the three children of General Amadeus Matsika have been raised behind barbed wire. They've never ridden on a bus or shopped in an open market. Then the oldest, thirteen-year-old Tendai, sneaks the others out of the compound to go on a Boy Scout trip, and they are immediately captured by the Great She Elephant and put to work in her plastics mine. Help is on the way because their mother has hired that intrepid team of expert mutant detectives, the Ear, the Eye, and the Arm, who can see, hear, and sense the intent of those around them.

119. Haddix, Margaret Petersen. *Among the Hidden*. Simon & Schuster, 1998. **M J**
Luke is a third—an illegal child. If the Population Police catch his family, the consequences are serious indeed. It has been easy to hide Luke for most of his twelve years, since the Garners are very careful and live in a wooded, isolated area. Then bulldozers appear nearby as the government starts building housing for the overcrowded cities. Luke, while peering out a vent, sees a girl at a neighboring property—how can this be? The family near the Garners already has two children besides her. When Luke begins sneaking out to meet this girl, he puts both the families into life-threatening danger. Sequel: *Among the Impostors*.

120. Hughes, Monica. *The Crystal Drop*. Simon & Schuster, 1993. **M J**
Water is precious in a future where a hole in the ozone layer has resulted in the greenhouse effect; now very little rain ever falls. When

their mother dies, thirteen-year-old Megan and her younger brother leave their drought-stricken farm to try to find their Uncle Greg. He is supposed to be living in a settlement out west near a waterfall. When these two children set out all alone to find their only remaining relative, they have no idea just how dangerous their journey will be.

121. Huxley, Aldous. *Brave New World*. Chatto & Windus, 1932. **J S**
     Along with *1984*, this classic work is a dystopian look at what the future has in store for humankind: test tube babies; no free will; the use of soma, a psychedelic drug, for social control; and the ever popular feelies, or virtual reality movies. In a carefully controlled future, once babies are decanted, chemicals are used during their developing years to see that they grow up to meet the current needs of society. There is no room for independence or free expression, as a young savage from the reservation discovers too late. Stability is everything, and the government and the mass media are there to keep it that way.

122. Kilworth, Garry. *The Electric Kid*. Orchard Books, 1995. **M J**
     Hotwire and Blindboy live at the dump. Hotwire is an electronics expert—she can fix anything mechanical—and Blindboy can hear virtually any noise, no matter how infinitesimal. In this futuristic Earth that is overwhelmed by pollution, rich people travel in skidders, vehicles that glide along the surface of the land. One day when Hotwire and Blindboy are out scavenging, a man watches Blindboy help a woman get the right key to her skidder. The two are abducted to go to work for Mouseman, an evil street person, and they pit their ingenuity against the established criminals.

123. Lawrence, Louise. *The Keeper of the Universe*. Houghton Mifflin, 1993. **M J**
     Music that soothes the savage beast is played by Galactic Controllers to keep the inhabitants of the planets calm, less violent, and nonaggressive. Unfortunately being subjected to this music also causes people to lose their self-will, originality, and creativity. Ben Harran is the one controller who refuses to follow this practice. Since his sector includes the Earth, humanity is safe until one of Ben Harran's planets blows itself up and he is put on trial by the other controllers. To help him with his defense, Ben Harran captures several inhabitants from Earth and other planets. He plans to use

them to prove his point that self-determination is better than complete control and that he is not guilty of genocide and culpable neglect. The trial is an important one, with the fate of Earth hanging in the balance.

124. Lindholm, Megan. *Alien Earth*. Bantam, 1992. **S**
The Arthroplana and the Beastships have been rescuing humans from the dying Earth and ferrying them to the planets Castor and Pollux. Part of the Conservancy for Humankind's plan is to arrest human development before puberty, skipping the messiness of adolescence, which, of course, keeps Earth people from ever becoming thinking, mature adults. Tug, the Arthroplana on the Beastship *Evangeline*, is the mechanical creature that controls the powerful ship—doing all her thinking for her and directing her in her tasks. Raef is hiding in the Beastship. Raef meets Connie, one of the deckhands onboard, and because he is a stowaway and not subject to the Conservancy's experiment of arresting development, he enters manhood with all emotional and physical faculties intact. The journey is one of discovery of both self and the true plans of the Conservancy. When the ship *Evangeline* shares in the liberating knowledge of what is really going on, look out: *Evangeline* enraged is a woman with whom to contend.

125. McDevitt, Jack. *Moonfall*. HaperCollins, 1998. **J S**
This combination science fiction, disaster, and political novel featuring the vice president of the United States is an unabashed paean to the U.S. space program and a whole lot of fun. A catastrophic, planet-threatening event is heralded by the arrival in the solar system of the comet Tomiko. The good news is that the comet is headed toward the moon rather than the Earth. The bad news is once it destroys the moon, a huge, Texas-sized piece of debris is headed straight toward the Earth, and if it hits, life will be terminated. The vice president was on the moon when the comet was first sighted and spearheaded the evacuation, risking his life in the process. He is on his way home to a world that would have been destroyed except for good old American ingenuity, the pig-headed refusal to admit defeat, and the ricochet effect.

126. Oppel, Kenneth. *Dead Water Zone*. Little, Brown, 1993. **J S**
In a bleak future, Paul gets a phone call from his missing brother who disappeared while doing research down at the piers. Sam wants

Paul to come to meet him in the Dead Water Zone. This is Paul's chance to find out what happened to his younger brother and also why it is not wise to drink the water in that area. Paul has no idea how dangerous his quest will be or just what is in store for him when he enters the Dead Water Zone.

127. Orwell, George. *1984*. Harcourt, 1949. **J S**
Big Brother is watching, and how. Winston Smith is a small-time bureaucrat who always does what is expected of him. Finally driven too far, he rebels against the dictatorship, but Big Brother and the Thought Police are too much for him. Winston's rebellion and sought-for freedom are tragically short lived, but the resulting picture of a dystopian society is one of the most influential and far-reaching works of science fiction in the twentieth century.

128. Pace, Sue. *The Last Oasis*. Delacorte, 1993. **J S**
In a world in which water is scarce and it's dangerous to go out without sunscreen, the mall is the safest place to be, particularly during the day. It is also an extremely dangerous place to try to live, as the three teenagers in this novel discover. They have heard a rumor that there are still hydroponics labs somewhere in Idaho. After the latest raid on the mall, the teens set out on a hazardous trip on the Snake River, desperately trying to reach this last oasis before it is too late.

129. Philbrick, Rodman. *The Last Book in the Universe*. Scholastic, 2000. **M J**
Spaz lives in the urbs, the polluted, gang-controlled cities filled with down-and-out characters who constantly use mind probes that rot their brains with chemically induced realities. Because of his epilepsy, Spaz can't use the probes and so can still reason. When he receives a visit from an illegal runner with a message that his little sister Bean is dying, he sets off to cross the forbidden boundaries of the urbs to see her one last time. Accompanied by an old man called Ryter, a little tyke who can't speak except for saying the word "Chox," and Lanaya, a princess of the proovs, Spaz finds that his journey encompasses much more than just a deathbed visit. Breathtakingly paced, inventive, and action packed, Philbrick's science fiction novel also asks classic questions about the nature of human beings and the future of this decaying planet.

130. Robinson, Kim Stanley. *Antarctica*. Bantam, Doubleday, Dell, 1998. **S**
This novel is an ecological thriller set in the twenty-first century; it is also a paean to the southernmost continent. The author went to Antarctica, courtesy of the National Science Foundation, and became fascinated with the mystique of this cold, barren, snow-locked landscape. As in his award-winning Mars trilogy, once again Robinson has brought humanity's efforts to tame an alien landscape stunningly to life, or in this case, to provide protection from human encroachment. The greenhouse effect is a very real concern of future scientists. Up until now, an international treaty has protected Antarctica from exploitation. The treaty is about to dissolve, and waiting in the wings are various oil companies, ready to move in and begin stripping away natural resources. Opposing them is a group of Earth First protectors who will do whatever it takes to keep the oil companies out, including committing murder.

131. Shusterman, Neal. *Downsiders*. Simon & Schuster, 1999. **M J**
At a time in the future, the forgotten subway tunnels built in 1867 under New York City are inhabited by people called Downsiders. Downsiders only surface topside for an emergency. Talon, a teen living in the underground community, risks going above for medicine for his sister and meets Lindsay, another teen. Talon violates the code of his community by bringing Lindsay below to show her the tunnels and networking of the downside. Chase, capture, and punishment for breaking the oath follows, but Talon continues using all his skills to remain both alive and a part of his underground family.

132. Sleator, William. *Others See Us*. Dutton, 1993. **M J**
Sixteen-year-old Jared is excited about spending his summer vacation with his family at their compound on the beach, especially with his beautiful cousin Annelise. After Jared falls into the swamp near his house, he can hear other people's thoughts, discovering to his shock that beautiful Annelise is not nearly as attractive on the inside as she is on the outside. In fact, Annalise is not even a very safe person to be around.

133. Turtledove, Harry. *The Case of the Toxic Spell Dump*. Pocket Books, 1993. **S**
Dave Fisher is an inspector for the Environmental Perfection Agency. Sent to investigate a report that the Devonshire dump is

leaking toxic spell components, Dave discovers that something is indeed up. There's an increased incidence of elf-shot victims, perhaps because larger numbers of pesky elves are being drawn by the power leaking out of the dump. Exorcisms are up as well, but the true horror is the increase in birth defects—three vampires, two lycanthropes, and three babies born without souls. It's Dave to the rescue in a humorous novel that features a bureaucrat as a most unlikely hero.

134. Ure, Jean. *Plague*. Harcourt, 1991. **M J**
Fran spends a month in the wilderness with a group of teachers and students, taking part in a survival program. When she returns home, she discovers that the city of London has been decimated by a mysterious plague. Fran is fortunate enough to find a couple of friends from school still alive, but will they stay that way as they try to make it safely out of the city?

Hackers and Droids

Computers rule! Virtual reality can be filled with electronic bugs, armies fighting each other to the death, or computermites advising Alice in her quest to solve the Jigsaw Murders.

135. Anthony, Piers. *Killobyte*. Putnam Penguin, 1992. **S**
   Killobyte is a seductive virtual-reality game based on the concept of kill or be killed. Players in this fantasy world see the blood, hear the death screams, and experience an adrenaline surge or the pain of death with each kill. One of the players, Baal Curran, a high school senior with juvenile diabetes since she was ten, is depressed enough to be thinking of suicide. Another player, Walter Toland, is a paraplegic ex-police officer, delighted to be able to walk and run again, courtesy of the game. The two meet and become friends while playing, only to have their lives threatened by a psychotic teenage hacker who plays the game for real.

136. Bova, Ben. *Death Dream*. Bantam Books, 1994. **S**
   Dan Santorini has moved his family to Florida because of his new job at Cyber World; he's designing a virtual reality theme park near Orlando. Then Dan learns that a program he and an old friend worked on in Ohio has developed a glitch and may be responsible for killing people. Dan is called in to investigate, but before he can make any headway, he is faced with another problem. His twelve-year-old daughter has been playing virtual reality games at her new school. This has made her vulnerable to manipulation by a man obsessed with young girls who happens to be Dan's new boss.

137. Cross, Gillian. *New World*. Holiday House, 1995. **M J**
     Miriam has nightmares, and Stuart is afraid of spiders. Both fourteen-
     year-olds have been hired to test a new experimental computer game
     that has been rigged to play on their fears so that the designer can test
     a new fail-safe device in the gloves the players wear. The teens also
     don't know that the designer's son, Will, is playing the game as well.
     Will is gleefully torturing the two sprites he sees on his computer
     screen, not realizing that they are real people suffering psychological
     torments as a result. When the teens discover what is going on, they
     work together to teach the designer a lesson—that playing on some-
     one's fears can be dangerous indeed.

138. Dick, Philip K. *Do Androids Dream of Electric Sheep?* Random
     House, 1981. **S**
     This is the science fiction classic that inspired the movie *Blade Run-
     ner*, a bleak, chilling picture of what is in store for humanity. Pollu-
     tion and radioactive fallout are such serious problems in the future
     that humans are encouraged to emigrate, bribed with ownership of a
     personal android servant if they do. Those left on Earth wear lead
     codpieces to protect their virility and take IQ tests to show that their
     intelligence hasn't dropped to below normal limits. If it does drop,
     they will be labeled as specials and will not be allowed to emigrate
     nor to have children. This is an Earth where possession of a live ani-
     mal is a status symbol, and those too poor to own one can pretend
     with electric animals (such as the sheep of the title). Rick DeCard is
     a bounty hunter who works for the San Francisco police department.
     His mission is to kill illegal androids posing as humans for a fee of
     $1,000 per body. There is a bitter taste left by the senselessness of it
     all. The androids fall to Rick's laser beams—but to what purpose, es-
     pecially when he winds up falling in love with an android himself? A
     disturbing picture of what the future may well bring to this overpop-
     ulated, resource-stripped planet.

139. Dunn, J. R. *This Side of Judgment*. Harcourt, 1994. **S**
     In a future reminiscent of *Blade Runner*, a technique has been devel-
     oped to implant computer chips successfully into human brains. After
     the operation, these chipheads can interact on the virtual realm. The
     human brain, unable to handle such an information overload for any
     length of time, begins shutting down, with disastrous results. Ross
     Bohlen, an agent for the Computer Subversion Strike Force, has
     killed his share of chipheads in the past; now he'd like to arrest them

instead. To do so, he has to fight against human treachery, political intrigue, and a brutal killer on the loose who also happens to be one of these cybernetically enhanced chipheads.

140. Friesner, Esther. *The Sherwood Game*. Baen, 1995. **S**
Carl Sherwood, software wizard at Manifest Inc., loves role-playing games and has created Sherwood Forest, where he goes to "buckle the swash" at every opportunity. Carl has risen through the ranks of his game to become Robin Hood's right-hand man. Then a colleague finds him using the terminal at work to play his game and insists on going into Sherwood with Carl. When the two enter the game together, this changes things and makes it possible for Robin Hood to escape and run amuck in the real world. Carl has to make the transition from computer geek to swashbuckling hero for victory to be assured.

141. Gibson, William. *Neuromancer*. Ace Books, 1984. **S**
This dark and disturbing work features a society devoted to getting high on alcohol and drugs. For the interface cowboys, however, getting high means interfacing with their computers, wiring themselves into a terminal, and riding the electronic pathways. Case was the very best of these interface cowboys, but this time his excursions into Earth's computer matrix were for the wrong people. Winner of the Hugo, the Nebula, and the Philip K. Dick Award, this work is acknowledged by many to be the seminal cyberpunk novel. Sequels: *Count Zero*; *Mona Lisa Overdrive*.

142. Goonan, Kathleen Ann. *Queen City Jazz*. TOR Books, 1994. **S**
When she was three years old, Verity was brought to Shaker Hill from Edgetown just outside Cincinnati. Although the Shakers were afraid of the enlivened city, they still took the little girl home to raise as their own. Even when nubs were discovered behind her ears, Verity was certified plague free at the mandatory examination, which meant that she could stay with the Shakers. Verity befriended Cairo, a stray dog, but concealed the fact that she could also communicate mentally with him. She also told no one of the bell that summoned her once a year to study the information cocoon in the library at Dayton. When the plague strikes her community, Verity goes to Cincinnati to look for the key to reviving her loved ones. This quest takes her into a surreal world of strong emotions, strange yearnings, and an immersion in jazz. Other Nanotech Cycle novels: *Mississippi Blues; Crescent City Rhapsody*.

143. Gresh, Lois H. and Robert Weinberg. *The Termination Node*. Ballantine Books, 1999. **S**
Lois Gresh, a computer specialist who designs tests for security loopholes, also writes suspense and science fiction stories. Robert Weinberg is a prolific writer of suspense, horror, and science fiction. Together these two writers have produced an incredible cyberthriller featuring the world of hackers versus suits and the code of free will versus the law, a thriller set against a backdrop of greed, avarice, theft, and murder. Judy Carmody, aka TerMight, is a hacker, one of the best in the business, so good that she helps banks spot flaws in their security systems. In fact, Judy's working in a bank when a hacker makes a massive withdrawal and then puts it all back. Judy is trying to find out who was responsible when two suits try to kill her. Judy escapes, but her landlord is dead and she is accused of his murder. When other high-powered hackers start turning up dead, it's Judy against the system. If she can just find the legendary Griswald, who disappeared a week ago, she might be able to survive. But if Griswald's working for the opposition, all is lost in this cyberhacker–techno-thrill ride of a novel.

144. Hogan, James P. *Bug Park*. Baen Books, 1997. **J S**
Fifteen-year-old Kevin Heber and his friend, Taki, have almost perfected a direct neural interface that allows them to actually exist in their Bug Park world in which they are the size of insects and motor around in tiny flying machines. Kevin's father, Eric, works for the tech company Neurodyne based in Tacoma, Washington. He has encouraged the teens to experiment with Neurodyne's newest DNC (direct neural coupling) that will replace the old virtual reality helmets once used by his company. Even Eric is unaware of the discoveries that Kevin and Taki have made. When Eric's second wife, the evil Vanessa, reveals herself as a corporate spy, Kevin takes a life-threatening chance as a mec, and in his DNC world, follows Vanessa to foil her murderous plans. Extremely inventive, with teen characters center stage.

145. Noon, Jeff. *Automated Alice*. Crown Books, 1996. **M J S**
Noon has brought Alice to the cyberworld, and he's done it with clever plotting, whimsical humor, and a cast of characters as intriguing as the original. Noon's Alice is at Great Aunt Ermintrude's house in Manchester, England, putting together a jigsaw puzzle of the London Zoo when her aunt's parrot, Whippoorwill, flies up the grandfa-

ther clock's case. Alice takes off in hot pursuit and lands in a nest of Computermites, then goes after the pieces of the puzzle as the Jigsaw Murders begin. She must solve numerous intellectual games before she can return in time for tea on a rainy afternoon. Alice also meets herself—her alter ego, a computer girl—in this Wonderland that often displays a hint of Lewis Carroll's, including an invisible cat named Quark. Charming, with puns galore and new illustrations that echo the classic drawings of Sir John Tenniel.

146. Rubinstein, Gillian. *Space Demons*. Dial Books, 1988. **M**
Andrew is a spoiled seventh-grade boy who gets a new computer game when his father comes back from Japan. Space Demons has no instructions with it, just pictures that show the various boards. Andy invites his best friend to join him in exploring this new game, and once they get to a certain level, Andrew discovers that he needs a third player. Since the program feeds on hate, Andy chooses the new girl in school and gives her something to hate—himself. By this time, he has become so obsessed with the game that he doesn't see the space demons when they first appear in real life. Not until the school bully is trapped inside the game does Andy realize just how dangerous life has become, both inside and outside the virtual reality realm. Sequel: *Skymaze*.

147. Scott, Michael. *Gemini Game*. Holiday House, 1997. **M J**
B. J. and Liz, fifteen-year-old twins who inherited the Gemini Corporation after their parents were killed, are game makers—creators of sophisticated, wildly popular virtual reality (VR) games. Unfortunately, a dozen people have gone into virtual reality comas while playing their latest game, Night's Castle. Captain Eddie Lyons is a twenty-year-veteran police officer in charge of the department that specializes in licensing and policing VR games. Lyons hates the twins, insists that Night's Castle is illegal, and plans to throw its creators into a virtual reality prison. B. J. and Liz escape to the Quays, a wild, lawless place where they can look for the flaw in the game, and risk everything by making one last trip into their game world before Captain Lyons closes his net on them.

148. Skurzynski, Gloria. *Virtual War*. Simon & Schuster, 1997. **M J**
Two teens, fourteen-year-olds Corgan and Sharla, and the young ten-year-old child, Brig, have been raised in isolation by the Federation. They have been trained according to their strengths to fight the Virtual

War, which will determine the future of human life on Earth. Eighteen days before the war is to begin, the three children meet each other, melding and molding their skills so that they act as one in the coming battle. Brig is the brilliant strategist who feeds information into Corgan's mind. Corgan is the soldier, the man of strength, and Sharla is the code breaker. The rules of the conflict are that each army can only protect its men, not advance. The three children must learn to trust each other and work together to forestall the end of civilization.

149. Stephenson, Neal. *Snow Crash*. Bantam Books, 1992. **S**
Snow Crash is a metavirus and an extremely destructive drug, crashing computers, putting hackers into comas or killing them, and spreading like wildfire. Hiro Protagonist, hacker extraordinaire and pizza deliverer nonpareil, has his hands full saving cybercivilization. Hiro's day job is to deliver pizza on time for CosaNostra Pizza, Inc. When an accident threatens to make him late, Y. T., a kourier from Radiks Radikal Kourier Systems who had harpooned his car with an electromagnet and was stealing a free ride on her skateboard, comes to Hiro's rescue and delivers the pizza on time. Hiro is also a member of Mr. Lee's Greater Hong Kong and is an expert at Japanese ceremonial sword fighting, both in the metaverse he helped to create and in the real world. When Snow Crash threatens both worlds, Hiro and Y. T. go after the organization responsible for its spread. Lots of humor, nonstop action, and lively dialogue in an irreverent, inspired narrative as these two teens save the world from the infocalypse.

150. Vande Velde, Vivian. *User Unfriendly*. Harcourt, 1991. **M J**
A group of eighth graders has managed to obtain a pirated copy of the Rasmussen program, a state-of-the-art interactive game that requires carefully controlled preparation and constant monitoring during play. Being typical teens, they ignore the safeguards and dive right in. Arvin Rizalli, the narrator, plays an elf in the game and is shocked to discover that the serving wench joining them is his mother. Felice had decided to surprise her son, but she is the one in for a surprise as she gets a headache that intensifies as the game progresses, threatening her with a stroke before the game ends. The boys are having fun fighting orcs, giant rats, river monsters, trolls, and others. Only when the program gets a glitch and they have no cleric to raise the dead do they discover that the dangers they are facing can be very real indeed.

Here There Be Dragons

Dragons are creatures of enormous beauty, powerful talents, and mystical legends. Whether they are center stage in these tales or are the soul mates and companions of humans, their breathtaking beauty and physical powers make them appealing to the fantasy reader.

151. Bertin, Joanne. *The Last Dragonlord.* St. Martin's Press, 1998. **S**
Linden Rathan is the Last Dragonlord. Known as Little One, he waits for a new dragonlord to appear that will hopefully be his soul mate. Linden is friends with the Bard Otter and has a magnificent Llysanyin stallion that understands everything his master says. Linden's latest mission is to accompany a soul-twinned pair of dragons to Cassori. The dragons are to sit in judgment as arbiters of the debate over who will be the next regent. Magic was used to sink the queen's barge, and her son is still too young to rule in her stead; there are two uncles capable of taking charge, however. Unfortunately for the Dragonlords, there is black magic afoot involving a plan to control the kingdom and destroy them, using blood practice and a soultrap jewel. During the course of this mission, Linden meets his soul mate, the young captain of her own ship, the *Sea Mist.* She belongs to a powerful merchant family and has as her enemy the noblewoman, Lady Sherrine, who wants Linden for herself. This is a lyrical romance, full of dragon lore and nefarious plots, with right triumphant in the end. Sequel: *Dragon and Phoenix.*

152. Fletcher, Susan. *Flight of the Dragon Kyn.* Simon & Schuster, 1997. **M J**
King Orrick believes that fifteen-year-old Kara can call the dragons. He wants her to summon them so that his warriors can then kill the

creatures; his lady, Signy, will not marry him until the dragons that killed her brother are punished. Kara does posses powers, but they allow her to call birds from the sky. Kara is abducted and taken to the king's steading. To test her powers, the king has Kara call falcons. Once Kara calls the dragons, they take her into their lair, but when she becomes familiar with their lives, she can't bring herself to complete her task. Prequel: *Dragon's Milk*. Sequel: *Sign of the Dove*.

153. Hambly, Barbara. *Dragonsbane*. Ballantine Books, 1985.
Dragon lore abounds in this fantasy featuring Jenny Waynest, a sorceress, and her love, John Aversin, called Dragonsbane because he is the only living man ever to slay a dragon. John's dragon-slaying skills are needed again because Merkeleb, the Black Dragon, has seized the Deep of Yeferdun. The king sends young Gareth to the far Winterlands to seek the help of Dragonsbane and Jenny, but their quest yields more than a dragon as the trio winds up facing the evils and snares set for them by the sorceress Zyerne. During the struggle, Jenny is torn between her love for John Aversin and their two sons and her desire to perfect her magic, especially after the magic and allure of the dragon enters her very soul. Sequels: *Dragonshadow*; *Knight of the Demon Queen*.

154. Kellogg, Marjorie B. *The Book of Earth: Volume One of the Dragon Quartet*. Daw Books, 1994. **S**
Four mighty dragons, the elemental energies of earth, water, fire, and air, were responsible for creating the world. Afterward they went to sleep, not to rise again until world's end. Suddenly the dragon Earth awakens in tenth-century Germany. Earth rescues fourteen-year-old Erde, who is hiding in a cave from witch hunters sent out by an evil priest. She is also hiding from her father's unwanted attentions. Erde bonds with the newly awakened dragon, which doesn't know why it has been summoned and can't remember how to use any of its powers—at least at first. Sequels: *The Book of Water: Volume Two of the Dragon Quartet*; *The Book of Fire: Volume Three of the Dragon Quartet*.

155. Kerner, Elizabeth. *Song in the Silence: The Tale of Lanen Kaeler*. TOR Books, 1997. **S**
When Lanen Kaelar of Kolmar inherits her adopted father's farm, Hadronsstead, for the first time in her life she can make her own decisions. Tied to the property all her young life, Lanen has dreamed of

sailing from Kolmar to the Dragon Isle, of adventuring far beyond her isolated youthful days. She leaves the farm to Walther, the neighboring lad who has looked after her, and makes her way first to the Great Fair at Illara and then to Corli and the ships that sail once a year to the Dragon Isle. Once Lanen reaches the island, the third-person narrative speaks in two voices, Lanen, and Kantri the dragon's. Lanen's fascination with the dragons began in her youth when she heard a traveling bard sing a dragon song, but the reality of meeting and saving the powerful race of dragons is not nearly so romantic. Neither a beauty nor a scholar, Lanen nevertheless has strange powers and an empathic understanding of dragon thought. Sequel: *The Lesser Kindred*.

156. McCaffrey, Anne. *The Dragonriders of Pern*. Random House, 1988. **J S**

This volume contains all three of the first Dragonrider novels. *Dragonflight* introduces Lessa, the sole survivor of the massacre of Ruatha Hold. She is rescued from servitude there by dragonriders searching for likely maidens able to impress the new queen dragon. Lessa succeeds in imprinting with Ramoth, which makes her the leader of the Weyr and the mate of F'lar, rider of bronze Mnementh, who is busy preparing the Weyr for the return of the deadly thread. *Dragonquest* is F'nor's story, the brother of F'lar and rider of the brown dragon Canth. When a few ambitious lords want one of the dragonriders to attempt to fly to the red planet and stop the thread before it falls, F'nor and Canth almost lose their lives by attempting the impossible. *The White Dragon* continues the Pern saga with the story of Jaxom, young lord of Ruatha Hold, who rescues the white dragon Ruth when she is trapped in her shell. Jaxom imprints with her and then learns that this runt of the litter possesses unique abilities that are sorely needed in the ongoing battle against the deadly thread.

157. McCaffrey, Anne. *Dragonseye*. Ballantine Books, 1996. **S**

The preparations that lead up to the second pass of thread on Pern are presented here. It has been two hundred and fifty years since the red star loomed large in the skies of Pern. The Weyrs have maintained order and discipline and are doing everything in their power to prepare their world for imminent thread fall. The holds have also been getting ready for the past two years, with one notable exception: Chalkin, Lord Holder of Bitra, not only refuses to believe in the rapidly approaching fall of thread but also keeps his people in ignorance, tithing for his own personal gain and condemning entire families to death by starvation and freezing cold in the coming harsh winter. A young artist naively accepts a commission to do miniatures of Chalkin's children and just barely escapes with his life. This is the catalyst that finally turns the rest of the holds against Chalkin and leads to his impeachment and the reestablishment of the rightful heir to hold leader. Strong characterization, vivid action scenes, and those wonderful telepathic dragons.

158. McCaffrey, Anne. *Dragonsong*. Simon & Schuster, 1983. **M J**
Fifteen-year-old Menolly, youngest daughter of the leader of Half Circle Hold, has a fascination with all things musical, which raises the ire of her parents. Since her father refuses to let any of the young men in the hold waste their time on music, Menolly helped the elderly harper, Petiron, and becomes in fact, if not in name, the harper's apprentice. Menolly is so talented that Petiron sends two of her songs to the masterharper, Robinton, but he dies before he can reveal the name of his new apprentice. While Robinton is searching all of Pern for the talented youngster who wrote these songs, Menolly is assigned to be music instructor of the hold children until the new harper comes. Menolly is savagely beaten by her father for absentmindedly strumming a few notes from one of her own songs and she is crippled deliberately by her mother. Forbidden all music and unable to play the way she could before, Menolly runs away. She finds a clutch of firedragon eggs, befriends the miniature queen, and when they hatch, impresses an unheard of nine firedragons and then teaches them how to harmonize to her songs. Menolly is rescued during threadfall by a dragonrider from Lessa's hold, is finally discovered by Robinton, and is taken to live and work at Harper Hall. Sequels: *Dragonsinger*; *Dragondrums*.

159. McKinley, Robin. *The Hero and the Crown*. Ballantine, 1986. **M J**
Aerin, daughter of the king of Damar, is passed over as the heir to the kingdom because she is thought to be tainted by the blood of her witchwoman mother. To prove her critics wrong, she finds a recipe for an ointment that will protect her against dragon burns, goes out to kill the small dragons infecting the realm, and earns the name Dragonslayer. To her surprise, she and her father's lame war steed are even successful against a monstrous dragon stirred up by the evil forces gathering in the north. But Aerin is mortally wounded, slowly dying until a dream leads her to a master mage who not only heals her but gives her the guidance she needs so that she and her magic blue sword, Gonturan, can rescue her kingdom from the forces of darkness

raised by the head of the huge dragon she had killed. Companion novel: *The Blue Sword.*

160. Murphy, Shirley Rousseau. *Nightpool.* HarperCollins, 1988. **M J**
Told in flashbacks, Prince Tebriel's tormented past is revealed—the disappearance of his mother, the murder of his father, and his own enslavement and torture at the hands of his father's murderer. Tebriel was kept alive because of the dragonbard mark on his arm, while his older sister was kept for breeding purposes. Tebriel was rescued by animals that could speak, the resistance forces rising up against the powers of the dark, and a newly awakened singing dragon. With no memory of what had happened, the boy took shelter with the otters. Now sixteen, Prince Tebriel decides to leave the safety of Nightpool, the otter colony that has been his home for the past four years, and go forth to battle the evil hydrus and find the singing dragon to go with the mark on his arm. Sequels: *The Ivory Lyre*; *The Dragonbards.*

161. Norton, Andre and Mercedes Lackey. *The Elvenbane: An Epic High Fantasy of the Halfblood Chronicles.* TOR Books, 1991. **S**
In the Chronicles, elvenlords rule over humans and half-breeds. They live in magnificent cities run by slaves and take as many women as they want as concubines. The story opens with Lord Dryan's concubine, Serina Daeth, out on the desert; she is pregnant and dying. Dragon Alara (in her midwife form) delivers Serina's child, Shana, and takes the half-breed girl to live with her in the dragons' lair. Shana is the fulfillment of the Prophecy, the Elvenbane who will spell the downfall of the elevenlords. Raised to believe herself a dragon, Shana does not learn of her prophetic task until much later. Alara treats Shana as she does her own child, Keman. However, the other dragons do not welcome Shana into their world and cast Shana out into the desert. A caravan finds her and she is taken as a concubine for Lord Bernel. Her brother, Keman, watches her, hoping to be able to rescue her. When the traders find Shana's mother's golden, jewel-encrusted slave collar, they know that Shana is no ordinary half-breed. Sequel: *The Elvenblood.*

162. Tolkien, J. R. R. *The Hobbit: Or There and Back Again.* G. Allen & Unwin, 1937. **M J**
What hobbits like best are tasty meals, a cozy chair by a warm fire, and a comfy home. When thirteen dwarves arrive at hobbit Bilbo

Baggins's house for dinner, they miraculously convince him to set off with them to recapture their treasure from the dragon, Smaug. Bilbo is to be the burglar of the company. Adventures along the way include meetings with trolls and orcs, attacks by giant spiders, and Bilbo's fortunate recovery of Gollum's magic ring. Written before his Lord of the Rings trilogy, this is Tolkien's classic quest novel that establishes beloved characters and the magical kingdom of Middle Earth. Although the confrontations with evil characters can be violent in *The Hobbit*, there are also some lighthearted, gently humorous scenes, unlike the trilogy that follows. A literate, engaging fantasy that can be read over and over again.

163. Vande Velde, Vivian. *Dragon's Bait*. Harcourt Brace, 1992. **M J**
Fifteen-year-old Alys is accused of being a witch, tied to a stake, and left as a sacrifice for the dragon. After working herself free, she realizes that she has no place else to go and there are wolves howling in the woods. Alys decides to accept her fate and get it over with quickly. The dragon ignores her, so she throws a rock at him to get his attention, shuts her eyes, and waits for the dragon to eat her. Instead, she is grabbed by the very human pair of hands of a young man with dragon eyes who is only two years older than she is. The shape-shifting dragon is intrigued by a young girl who attacks instead of acting as a victim, so he offers to help her get revenge. Alys gladly accepts, but she soon discovers that revenge can be a two-edged sword, not nearly as satisfying in reality as in her dreams. Bright dialogue, lots of action, a very satisfying love story, and something to think about as well.

164. Wrede, Patricia C. *Dealing with Dragons*. Harcourt, 1990. **M J S**
The first book of the *Enchanted Forest Chronicles* is a witty, clever spoof of fairy tales and dragon lore. It introduces Princess Cimorene, who was not cursed at her christening, is taller than most princesses, and is bored by embroidery but loves dueling, Latin studies, and other things her stuffy parents claim are not appropriate for a princess. When the royal parents introduce Cimorene to the dull, stodgy suitor they have picked out for her, the headstrong princess runs away, knocks on a dragon's cave, and becomes the willing servant of the dragon Kazul. When handsome princes come to rescue her, she sends them elsewhere. Cimorene is too busy studying magic, melting wizards, and helping her female dragon become king of the Dragons. A light, frothy, diverting fantasy that is

followed by three more, all just as much fun. Sequels: *The Enchanted Forest Chronicles: Searching for Dragons*; *Calling on Dragons; Talking to Dragons.*

165. Yep, Laurence. *Dragon War*. HarperCollins, 1992. **M J**
Shimmer, the dragon princess, along with her companions Monkey and Indigo, attempt to rescue Thorn, Shimmer's human friend, whose soul has been imprisoned in the Boneless King's cauldron. The Boneless King is too powerful for them, so the three journey to the high king of the dragons to ask for help. The Boneless King's evil plan is to boil the seas with the cauldron and thus destroy the dragons' underwater home. Shimmer's brother, Pomfret, allies himself with the wicked king, forcing Shimmer to fight against her own kind. This is the fourth volume in Yep's series. Prequels: *Dragon of the Lost Sea*; *Dragon Steel*; *Dragon Cauldron.*

166. Yolen, Jane. *Dragon's Blood*. Delacorte, 1982. **M J**
This first novel in *The Pitdragon Trilogy* introduces Jakkin Stewart, a young bondsman on a worm farm, where dragons are bred and raised to fight in the gaming pits. Jakkin has a plan that he hopes will gain him his freedom. He plans to steal a dragon hatchling, raise it, and train it to fight. This is taking a chance, since there are severe penalties for anyone caught stealing a dragon. And not all dragons turn out to be first-class fighters; not everyone who tries to train them has the fight for it or the ability to mind bond with these great worms. Jakkin's bond with Heartsblood, the baby dragon he obtains, is truly extraordinary, as are the adventures that the two have together. Sequels: (*The Pitdragon Trilogy*) *Heartsblood*; *A Sending of Dragons.*

167. Yolen, Jane. *Here There Be Dragons*. Harcourt Brace, 1993. **M J**
Yolen's fascination with dragons is clear. In these eight stories and five poems, she explores dragon lore that is gory, humorous, lighthearted, and evil. Some of the entries are inspired by folklore, such as Arthurian stories, and some are simply the creation of a vivid imagination. Each selection is prefaced by Yolen's brief introduction explaining why, when, or how the selection came to be, and the drawings complement the text perfectly, lending an element of mystery and awe.

Imagination's Other Place

These stories speak of other worlds that have unique flora and fauna, placcs of fragile beauty or malevolent evil, magical lands that exist only in the author's imagination.

168. Askounis, Christina. *The Dream of the Stone*. Farrar, Straus, & Giroux, 1993. **M J**
Fifteen-year-old Sarah's parents are killed when they attempt to rescue her brother, Sam, from the research institute called CIPHER. Sarah and a handsome gypsy boy named Angel Muldoon work together to rescue Sam and to find the stone talisman that will aid them in their quest to rid the earth of the cosmic evil, the Umbra.

169. Barnes, John. *One for the Morning Glory*. TOR Books, 1996. **J S**
This lighthearted fantasy spoof begins when two-year-old Prince Amatus gets into the wine of the gods and becomes just half a person as a result—literally. Everything to the left of the bridge of his nose, from top to bottom, simply disappears. Amatus's father has the four responsible for the prince's safety beheaded, but then he needs a new personal maid, royal alchemist, royal witch, and captain of the guard. A year and a day later, the prince's new caretakers show up: the alchemist Golias, Mortis the witch, the heavily cloaked and disguised Twisted Man as captain of the guards, and a young girl, Psyche, as the personal maid. And so Amatus grows up, surrounded by friends and followers who love him. A daring young man in spite of his disability, Amatus sets himself quests, even going underground to the goblin kingdom to rescue a kidnapped maid. Unfortunately, Golias the alchemist is killed on this expedition, but Amatus gains his left foot, a

clear indication that only with the sacrifice of his other companions will he become whole again. There are battles galore and even a tender romance in this humorous, diverting, fast-paced fantasy romp.

170. Britain, Kristen. *Green Rider*. Penguin Putnam, 1998. **S**
This debut fantasy begins with the young girl Karigan unjustly kicked out of school for standing up to a bully who just happened to be the heir of the lord-governor of Mirwell province. Karigan's father, although wealthy, was only a merchant. Returning home through the forest, she encounters a dying Green Rider. Impaled by two black-shafted arrows, the Rider makes Karigan swear on his sword to deliver the life-and-death message he carries for the king. He also gives her his golden-winged horse brooch, the sign of his office; warns her to "Beware the Shadow Man"; and dies. Before long, Karigan discovers firsthand just how deadly the Shadow Man and his minions can be. Fortunately, the spirit of the slain rider follows behind, ready to guard and protect her and foil the evil spread by the Shadow Man. When Karigan finally delivers the message to the king, she discovers that this is only the beginning as she is called on to join the Green Riders in their efforts to save both liege and kingdom from the encroaching dark. This richly textured fantasy is full of deeds of derring do, battles, magic, mayhem, romance, and animal-human bonding as Karigan forms a very special relationship with the dead rider's horse.

171. Brooks, Terry. *Magic Kingdom for Sale—Sold!* Del Ray, 1986. **J S**
While still grieving for his deceased wife, wealthy Ben Holiday sees an ad in a catalogue offering a magic kingdom for sale. For just one million dollars, he can purchase Landover, enchanted home of knights and knaves, dragons and damsels, wizards and warlocks. Ben is intrigued and signs on the dotted line. When he arrives in Landover, he is met by Questor Thews, chief advisor to the throne of Landover and wizard of the court—who is extremely inept at the practice of magic. Ben's castle, Sterling Silver, is tarnished and neglected because no king has been in residence for the past twenty years. Ben is now the king, but where are his subjects? To woo them back, he must trick a witch and a dragon, fight a demon lord, bring back the king's paladin and accept the sylph Willow's love. The first in the author's popular Landover series, this is a lighthearted, tongue-in-cheek fantasy quest adventure. Sequels: *The Black Unicorn*; *Wizard At Large*; *The Tangle Box*; *Witches' Brew*.

172. Bujold, Lois McMaster. *The Spirit Ring*. Baen Books, 1992. **J S**
Fiametta, the daughter of Prospero Beneforte, master of magic arts, serves as her father's assistant. Having learned from his example how to practice magic on her own, Fiametta creates a ring using the true-love spell of the master of Cluny. When Duke Ferrante and the evil sorcerer Vitelli attack the kingdom, it is this ring and the love it represents that enable Fiametta to bring a giant statue of Perseus to life and defeat the forces of evil threatening her country.

173. Bull, Emma. *Finder*. TOR Books, 1995. **J S**
Bull sets her murder mystery with a dark twist in that in-between zone of Borderland, a place of misfits, magics, and designer drugs. The finder of the title—Orient—and his partner, Tick-Tick, are after the murderer of a dealer. Someone is selling Passport to humans, claiming that it transforms them into elves. Problem: Passport is killing humans, not changing them. Filled with quirky characters and down-and-out settings, Bull intrigues the reader with her off-beat "who done it?" urban fantasy.

174. Calhoun, Dia. *Aria of the Sea*. Winslow Press, 2000. **M J**
Cerinthe's greatest wish is that she might be accepted at the School of the Royal Dancers. When her audition doesn't go well, she thinks she's been rejected and takes a position in the laundry room just to be near the famous teachers. Somehow, she hopes to secure a place alongside the haughty Elliana, another student who constantly taunts and challenges Cerinthe. When Cerinthe finally gets her wish and begins training for a starring role in a dance production, she no longer hears the singing of the Sea Maid, her beloved guiding force. Cerinthe's other talent is that of a healer, which she gave up when she failed to save her mother's life. Locked in a battle with Elliana for both star status and power in the school, Cerinthe must sort out her own path to the future. Calhoun's lyrical writing, the magical kingdom of Windward, and Cerinthe's enchanting personality make this novel one of the best of the year 2000 fantasy titles.

175. Charnas, Suzy McKee. *The Kingdom of Kevin Malone*. Harcourt, 1993. **M J**
Amy is dragged against her will into the fantasy world of Kevin Malone. He is the childhood bully who once stole from her but now needs her help. To escape from his abusive, alcoholic father, Kevin has created the Fayre Farre, a magic kingdom. Now Kevin is in danger and

needs three princesses to recover his magic sword, Farfarer. That's
how Amy and two of her friends become involved, entering Kevin's
kingdom on a quest fraught with danger from the Tolkien-like creatures created out of Kevin's abused-childhood fears.

176. Cherryh, C. J. *Rider at the Gate.* Warner Books, 1995. **S**
The creator of the Merchanter and Chanur universes has written a fantasy set on a primitive land where commerce and protection depend on
the good will of nighthorses and their riders. It is these bonded pairs
that go out into the wilds hunting for food and accompanying convoys
to keep them safe on long mountain treks. They also serve as a barrier
between human settlements and the creatures of the forests, from tiny
wally-boos willy-wisps to fierce predators such as the goblin cats
whose telepathic sendings can drive unprotected humans insane.
Danny Fisher is a headstrong young rider with a high-strung horse,
Cloud. Two years ago, this untamed horse showed up from the high
country and claimed the merchant's son as his own. Danny provides
much-needed funds to his pious parents, who nevertheless do not ap-
prove of his new endeavors. To make matters worse, the only rider
who was ever kind to Danny has lost his partner to a rogue, has been
himself accused of going rogue, and has been driven out of the village.
Danny follows him to the highlands as he searches for the rogue who
killed his partner. They are not alone. In pursuit are two parties, one
that ostensibly wants to help and the other that wants Danny's friend
dead. Young Danny and Cloud are caught in the middle. Once again
Cherryh has captured the sense of alienation and longing to fit in of a
talented loner struggling to come of age. Sequel: *Cloud's Rider.*

177. Chetwin, Grace. *The Chimes of Alyafaleyn.* Simon & Schuster, 1994.
M J
In the land of Alyafaleyn, people bond with beautiful golden spheres
called heynim when they are old enough to control them. Tambourel
is a youth with a special affinity for these spheres, but he is unable to
snare any for himself. One night Tambourel sneaks out to watch a
renowned healer trying to save the life of his best friend's mother in
the throes of childbirth. He is so close that he inadvertently becomes
a part of the healing process and is deeply affected by the harmonics
of the spheres. The old man leaves a gift for the baby he has saved, a
small golden heynim in a special box. Tambourel becomes her protector, and when she runs away, it is Tambourel, the heynless wonder,
who goes after her.

178. Hite, Sid. *Answer My Prayer*. Henry Holt, 1995. **J S**
Lydia lives in Jeefwood Forest, which is managed by her father for
the artisan guild. This year Lydia goes with her family on their yearly
trip to the harvest's end celebration at the seaside village of Valerton,
and there she falls in love at the artisan guild dance with Aldersan
Hale, Valerton's premier artist. Aldersan dances once with her and
promises her another, but he can't do so because a storm ends the
dance prematurely. Lydia returns to the forest and prays that Aldersan
will remain healthy and remember his promise—that's when an extremely lazy young guardian angel enters the picture. It should have
been simple for the angel Ebol to see that Lydia's prayer is answered,
but Aldersan gets caught up in a treasonous plot that only an angel
could straighten out.

179. Huff, Tanya. *Sing the Four Quarters*. Daw Books, 1994. **S**
Annice is a bard who can sing the four quarters and communicate
with the spirits of earth, air, fire, and water. She is also a royal
princess and has not spoken to her brother, King Theron, in ten years,
not since their father granted the deathbed request that allowed her to
become a bard and saved her from the marriage Theron had arranged.
Immediately after their father's death, the furious new king stripped
his sister of all royal privileges and warned her that if she ever became
pregnant, it would be considered an act of treason, leading to the execution of both mother and child. Now Annice is pregnant and the father of her baby has just been imprisoned. She knows that the charges
of treason are false, but Duc Pjerin has still been condemned to die.
To save herself and her baby, Annice must break Duc Pjerin of jail,
pregnant as she is, and help clear his name. Companion Novels: *Fifth
Quarter*; *No Quarter*; *The Quartered Sea*.

180. Ibbotson, Eva. *The Secret of Platform 13*. NAL, 1998. **M**
On Platform 13 in an old abandoned part of the railway station, there
is a door to a magical island filled with talking beasts, elves, and wizards. This door opens only once every nine years for nine days. Re-
grettably, the prince of the magical kingdom was with his nurse outside the door, visiting the real world of London, when he was
kidnapped by the greedy Mrs. Trottle. By the time the king and queen
realized that the prince was gone, the door was closed. It's a nine-year
wait before the rescue party can be sent out. Odge Gribble, an old hag;
Cor, the wizard; Burkie, the fey; and Hans, the ogre are selected to
find the prince. Once in London, they discover that the child (now

almost ten years old) Raymond Trottle is hardly worth rescuing—he's such a nasty boy. But aided by the Trottle's sweet kitchen boy, Ben (who, of course, is the real prince) they avidly pursue their goal. For younger teens, this lighthearted read pokes fun at family relationships and naughty children.

181. Jordan, Sherryl. *Winter of Fire*. Scholastic, 1993. **M J**
Elsha is a child of the Quelled, the slaves branded at age five, and must dig for firestones in the mines until they die. Elsha has spirit and defiance in her soul, however. She almost dies on her sixteenth birthday when she slacks in carrying stones up from the mine. As her punishment, a guard of the Chosen has increased her workload to the point of death. This is the day of the Festival, and miraculously, Elsha meets a Chosen called Amasi, the Firelord's steward. He says that Elsha is to leave her tasks and journey with him to become the Firelord's Handmaiden. Never before has a Quelled been allowed to live amongst the Chosen, let alone be a part of the all-powerful Firelord's household. Without the Firelord's power to divine where the firestones are, this icy rock-strewn earth would freeze and die. Elsha's elevation to Handmaiden does not come easily, however. When the Firelord dies, Elsha must battle the forces of the Chosen to convince them to allow her to take her place as the new Firelord. Often bleak yet written with power and compassion, Jordan's fantasy presents the ultimate outsider in Elsha, a woman who rises above a myriad of impediments to claim her place in society.

182. Kerr, Peg. *Emerald House Rising*. Warner Books, 1997. **S**
After the Founder's War, all the nobility of the city of Piyar are wary of using any magical talents. Collas the gem cutter works for the nobility, cutting and crafting magic amulets and precious jewelry. Jena, his daughter, is also a talented gem worker, having learned much from her father, but in this society, women are not expected to learn a skill but to marry and raise a family. When Lord Morgan, a noble from court, commissions a new ring from Collas, Jena's magical powers begin to surface. Morgan soon disappears. Jena consults the magician Arikan about the stone left in her father's care. Jena allies herself with Morgan's aunt to rescue the missing lord, and along the way, Jena hones her forbidden magical talents as well as her artistry as a gem cutter.

183. LeGuin, Ursula. *A Wizard of Earthsea*. Bantam, 1975. **M J S**
Sparrowhawk journeys to Gont Island as an apprentice to the Master

Wizard at Roke. Wizard Ogion the Silent molds the young mage, instructing him in chanting, the arts of weather, tricks of illusion, and spells of changing. Sparrowhawk, arrogant and proud, attempts a summoning spell before he is capable of controlling his powers, causing a rent in the fabric of time and unleashing a deadly evil. This is the first of four superbly written novels. Sequels: *The Tombs of Atuan*; *The Farthest Shore*; *Tehanu: The Last Book of Earthsea*.

184. McKenzie, Ellen Kindt. *The Golden Band of Eddris*. Henry Holt, 1997. **M J**
McKenzie's first novel combines magic, likable young protagonists, and a mysterious fantasy setting where sorcerers and knights do battle for control of the world. As the story opens, Anna is recounting tales of the Knights of Anla to her two children, Keld and Elylden. That night, Keld sees the troop of knights descend through their isolated woods. In the morning, Anna mysteriously sends both children away from the valley—Keld with his father's ring, Elyl with Anna's gift of foreseeing the future. The children are to journey alone to the city of Adnor, find a blind potter, and make connections with their other relatives. Keld and Elyl's journey to Adnor parallels Anna's pilgrimage to the cavern in the black mountains. There Anna faces the evil witch, Eddris, who is angry with Anna and determines to kill Keld and Elyl. Anna takes Eddris's Golden Band and gives it to her father, the wizard Stilthorn. Stilthorn can limit Eddris's deeds by simply possessing the band. Through powerful sorcery, Stilthorn aids the children in their quest to return this kingdom to the side of good. A well-plotted fantasy that combines elements of medieval quest tales with the magic of witches and wizards.

185. McKillip, Patricia. *Winter Rose*. Ace Books, 1996. **S**
In a lush, sensual retelling of Snow White and Rose Red, the two sisters Laurel and Rois Melior are entranced by the long absent and recently returned Corbet Lynn, whose family has been cursed for three generations. When the tale opens, practical Laurel is betrothed to Perrin, and romantic Rois is mesmerized by the handsome Corbet, who has returned to Lynn Hall to restore the decrepit mansion. The house is deep in the woods, and legend has it, was the scene of a vile murder—Nial Lynn, Corbet's grandfather, was supposedly killed by his own son, Tercel. In Rois's mystical attraction to the wilds, to brambles of roses, to the strange well on Corbet's property, and her hypnotic attraction to Corbet himself, McKillip lays the foundation for a dark, violent fairy tale for mature teens.

186. Nix, Garth. *Sabriel*. HarperCollins, 1996. **M J S**
Though she is the daughter of the necromancer Abhorsen and marked
with the charter as a mage, Sabriel lives not in the Old Kingdom with
her father but in the nonmagical Ancelstierre at Wyverley, where she
attends school with ordinary children. One night, a creature breaks
through from the world of the dead that brings Sabriel her father's
necromancer tools of bells and sword, and Sabriel must set off to rescue her father before he crosses the final gate into the underworld.
Dark, threatening evil permeates this tale. Sabriel must pit all her
skills against the creatures of death to prevail against the forces that
have swept her father into the river of death and beyond the gates of
redemption. Companion novel: *Lirael, Daughter of the Clayr*.

187. Nodelman, Perry and Carol Matas. *Of Two Minds*. Simon & Schuster,
1995. **M J**
This is not your ordinary prince and princess story. In Gepeth, all the
citizens have the ability to make worlds real through their imagina-
tions. Wisely, none use this power except the bored and rebellious
teen Princess Lenora. Her parents have betrothed her to Prince Coren
of Andilla. He wants nothing more than reality because his people
have the ability to mindread, a talent the prince doesn't much value.
Coren appears in Lenora's imagined world, and at the hasty marriage
ceremony, the two are transported to Lenora's imagined kingdom of
Grag. In Grag, the two teens have no powers, and the evil leader,
Hevak, has his own nefarious plans for the royal pair. Sequels: *More
Minds*; *A Meeting of the Minds*.

188. O'Donohoe, Nick. *The Magic and the Healing*. Ace Books, 1994. **S**
A group of veterinary students are asked to do a traveling rotation
with a favorite professor. Their destination comes as a complete surprise to everyone as they cross over into a fantasy land where they are
asked to treat the very real ailments of its denizens—unicorns,
griffins, and other mystical beasts. B. J. Vaughan is one of these students; she has just discovered that she has a terminal disease and she
contemplates suicide so that the disease will not reach its final, extremely painful stage. When B. J. enters the world of Crossroads,
however, she discovers that there is healing in the air, and before long
her symptoms have disappeared. It looks like B. J. isn't going to die
after all, provided she survives the final battle against the vicious
wolf-like Wyr. Sequels: *Under the Healing Sun*; *The Healing of
Crossroads*.

189. Pierce, Meredith Ann. *The Darkangel*. Little, Brown, 1982. **M J S**
The slave girl Aeriel follows her beautiful mistress, Eoduin, up the mountain to gather hornbloom nectar for a village wedding when the vampire Darkangel suddenly appears and spirits Eoduin away. No one in the village will dare challenge the vampire, so Aeriel sets out up the mountain alone to rescue her mistress. Darkangel takes Aeriel as well, though she is too ugly to be his bride. He only takes one bride a year, and he drinks the girl's blood, eats her heart, and wears her soul in a special necklace that contains the souls of all his previous brides. Darkangel wants Aeriel as a servant to the thirteen wraiths in his castle, all that is left of his brides, including Eoduin. Falling under the spell of the vampire's beauty herself, Aeriel tells him a story that upsets him so greatly that he decides to kill her. She escapes with the help of the castle's treasure keeper, who tells her how to find the blade adamant to use against Darkangel. When Aeriel returns with the blade, the vampire selects her to be his fourteenth and final bride before taking over the world. Sequels: *A Gathering of Gargoyles*; *The Pearl of the Soul of the World*.

190. Reichert, Mickey Zucker. *Beyond Ragnarok. The Renshai Chronicles: Volume One*. Daw Books, 1995. **J S**
This is a continuation of the Last of the Renshai trilogy, but it can be read and enjoyed on its own since Reichert provides an extensive prologue with all the necessary background information. Three hundred years have passed since the hero stood up to Odin and saved mankind and a few elves. The Renshai descendants of that hero now face a serious problem. Magic is loose in the land again, and the balance between law and chaos, long protected by the rulers of Bearn, is in danger. The king is dying and the Test of Staves given to his heirs to select the next ruler reveals that not a single one is worthy. One heir, however, remains untested, the child of the king's youngest son, banished years ago. Messengers sent to bring the boy to court are attacked and killed by magic. Hence the quest, undertaken by the king's favorite granddaughter; her lifelong companion, the son of the royal bard; Kevral, a young female Renshai warrior assigned to protect her; Ra-Khir, a young knight-in-training; and Tae, a young thief who overhears their plans and insists on going with them. There is wonderful world building here as well as magical battles, sympathetic characters, and lots of edge-of-seat suspense as these companions struggle to put an innocent on the throne. Sequels: *Prince of Demons*; *The*

Children of Wrath. Prequels: *The Last of the Renshai*; *The Western Wizard*; *Child of Thunder*.

191. Smith, Sherwood. *Crown Duel*. Harcourt, 1997. **M J**
     When their father dies, Meliara and her brother, Branaric, become the ruling family of Tlanth. They are severely impoverished, however, and do not have the money to pay the taxes due on the castle—taxes owed to the evil ruler of Remalna, Galdran. Mel and Bran lead a revolt against the power-hungry Galdran. He has broken the Covenant, the sacred agreement with the Hill Folk who provide the kingdom with the fire sticks that keep all warm in foul weather. Mel is no shy countess; she actively engages in the battle plans and her life is in danger during the conflict. Sequel: *Court Duel*.

192. Stevenson, Laura. *The Island and the Ring*. Houghton Mifflin, 1991. **S**
     The Princess Tania's island kingdom has almost been destroyed by the evil Lord Ascanet, with his warriors, called the silver souls, and his monstrous hippogriffs. Tania escapes the conflict, however, and has acquired the star sapphire ring that is the key to saving her beloved island. Tania and the severely scarred musician, Eliar, have a respite from the fighting in the Valley of Descaria but must ultimately face Ascanet to wrest control of the island back. Stevenson presents a strong woman protagonist who must face her own fears as she sets out on her quest to regain her kingdom.

193. Tolkien, J. R. R. *The Lord of the Rings*. Allen & Unwin, 1955. **M J S**
     Tolkien's sweeping, epic fantasy was originally published as three separate novels (*The Fellowship of the Ring*, *The Two Towers*, and *The Return of the King*). Set in his imaginary Middle Earth and peopled with elves, dwarves, hobbits, sorcerers, orcs, and a myriad of evil creatures, this serious quest saga begins with the wizard Gandalph visiting the hobbit Frodo Baggins, Bilbo's nephew. Gandalph informs Frodo that Bilbo's magic ring is the One Ring of Power, a ring that Sauron, the evil sorcerer, has forged. In the company of his loyal friend, Sam Gamgee, and others, Frodo sets out for Mount Doom in Mordor, determined to return the ring to its baptismal fire, thus destroying its nefarious powers. Pursued by ring wraiths called Nazguls and other dark creatures as well as the insane Gollum, Frodo attempts to complete his task. Few fantasy worlds are as enchanting or complete as Middle Earth; *The Lord of the Rings* can be perused many times in a reader's lifetime, each time with renewed pleasure and new insights.

194. Turner, Megan Whalen. *The Thief.* Greenwillow, 1996. **M J S**
Why take a thief out of prison only to employ him to steal? Gen
claims he can steal anything—and has landed in the king of Sounis's
prison for his activities. Gen considered his imprisonment an impossible situation to change until the king's magus removes him from his
jail—so that Gen may steal again! This time, Gen's task is set by the
king himself: he is to retrieve a precious gem from an ancient temple.
Gen isn't sent alone to accomplish this impossible task—the magus
and others are along to guard him, and the king has posted a tremen-
dous award of gold for Gen should he think of stealing the jewel for
himself and disappearing. A finely written fantasy/mystery, set in an
imaginary world that resembles ancient Greece in the time of warring
city-states. Sequel: *The Queen of Attolia.*

195. Voigt, Cynthia. *On Fortune's Wheel.* Simon & Schuster, 1991. **M J S**
Fourteen-year-old Birle, the innkeeper's daughter, is to marry the
huntsman Muir. Strangely enough, she finds a young man, Orien,
making off with the inn's boat, joins him, falls in love during their idle
down the river, and stays with Orien until they are captured and sold
into slavery. Orien is no ordinary man: He's a prince. Along with
Yula, the giant, whom they've met in their river journey, the three begin harsh lives, Orien at hard labor. Voigt weaves a tale of romance
and rescue, as Birle and Yul seek their own freedom and Prince
Orien's return to his rightful place. Prequel: *Jackaroo.* Sequels: *The
Wings of the Falcon; Elske.*

In Legendary Camelot

The cast is all here: Merlin the wizard extraordinaire, Guinevere the queen, Lancelot the warrior-lover, the Knights of the Round Table, and the legendary ruler, Arthur. Some of these Arthurian tales are told with magic and mystery, some are psychological studies, and some are simply adventure stories that keep the reader's heart pounding.

196. Barron, T. A. *The Lost Years of Merlin*. Putnam, 1996. **M J**
This first volume of a series about Merlin begins when a young boy with no name or memory washes ashore on the coast of Wales. To find out who he is, the boy must travel to the lost island of Fincayra, which serves as a bridge between the Earth of humans and the Otherworld of spiritual beings. Once on the island, the boy must accomplish various tasks and face the evil Rhita Gawr before learning the truth about his parents. In the end, having gained his name and some knowledge of who and what he is, Merlin is ready to take a central role in the Arthurian opus. Sequels: *The Seven Songs of Merlin*; *The Fires of Merlin*; *The Mirror of Merlin*; *The Wings of Merlin*.

197. Bradley, Marion Zimmer. *The Mists of Avalon*. Alfred A. Knopf, 1982. **S**
The Arthurian cycle is revisited in this novel but with a distinctly feminist slant. The heroine is Morgan le Fay, who in this version is not Arthur's enemy. Instead, Morgan sees the fate foretold for Arthur and for Merlin but is powerless to stop it. The emphasis here is on the conflict between the dying pagan beliefs of Morgan's people and the rapidly growing antifeminine beliefs of the followers of Christianity.

198. Bradley, Marion Zimmer. *The Forest House*. Viking, 1994. **S**
     In the tradition of *The Mists of Avalon* (see no. 147), Bradley has re-
     visited early Britain to give an account of the final days of the druidic
     priestesses in the Forest House. The narrator is Caillean, an unwanted
     girl-child in Hibernia across the sea. Brought to the Forest House by
     the priestess of the oracle, she rises to power and stands next to the
     high priestesses. One of these, Eilan, the greatest high priestess of all,
     falls in love with the Roman Gaius and has a child by him. That child,
     Gawan, becomes her people's hope for the future and must be saved
     in the end by his mother's willing sacrifice. Sequel: *Lady of Avalon*.

199. Cornwell, Bernard. *The Winter King*. St. Martin's Press, 1996; *En-
     emy of God*. St. Martin's Press, 1997; *Excalibur*. St. Martin's Press,
     1998. **S**
     Warlords indeed people this brutal and gory version of the Arthurian
     legend that depicts the clash between invading Saxons and native
     Britons as well as the religious struggle among Celtic paganism,
     Druids, and Christianity. All three novels are told in flashback by
     Arthur's warrior Derfel Cadarn, now a humble monk, a man of
     staunch loyalty, and at one time, fierce battle skills. *The Winter King*
     begins by following Arthur's travails to consolidate power for the
     infant Mordred, the proper king of Dumnonia, and adds layers of
     political and romantic intrigue by introducing the wily Merlin and
     the manipulative Guinevere. Arthur has become the enemy of God
     in the second part of this rousing trilogy in which the crafty Merlin
     leads the warriors on dark and blood-soaked pagan journeys to re-
     capture the Thirteen Treasures of Britain. Arthur is also betrayed
     here by the Isis-worshipping Guinevere and the sly, faithless
     Lancelot—hardly the romantic duo of more chivalric Camelot sto-
     ries. In the finale, *Excalibur*, Arthur is reconciled with his tarnished
     queen, while Derfel's account of his sacrifices for his beloved
     Ceinwyn include some of the most harrowingly brutal scenes in this
     masterful series. Lengthy but riveting.

200. Crompton, Anne Eliot. *Gawain and Lady Green*. Donald I. Fine
     Books, 1997. **S**
     Gawain, one of King Arthur's knights, rides into Holy Oak village
     during May Day festivities and is crowned king. There follows an
     idyllic period of romance with the Lady Gwyneth until Gawain real-
     izes that the May King's reward at harvest's end is not what he had
     thought. From Holy Oak, the tale shifts back to King Arthur's court,

where a giant green knight issues a challenge that Gawain takes up. This lilting retelling of the Gawain legend blends both sensuality and fierce violence.

201. Lawhead, Stephen R. *Taliesin. Book One of the Pendragon Cycle.* William Morrow, 1989. **M J S**
This dual narrative features Charis, princess of Lost Atlantis, and Taliesin, found as an infant in the freezing cold weir by a man who sees his luck change dramatically when he adopts the infant. Charis writes of their adventures as she lies in bed, waiting for their son Merlin to be born. As a young girl, Charis danced in the bullring of the Royal Temple of the Sun. After seven years she foresaw the impending doom of her world and led her family to safety across the sea. There she met Taliesin, a king's son but a barbarian in the eyes of her family. Her father, now the Fisher King, was against their union, but Charis responded to Taliesin's love and became his Lady of the Lake. If it hadn't been for the enmity of Morgian, her stepsister, their life together would have been perfect. Sequels: *Merlin*; *Arthur*.

202. McCaffrey, Anne. *Black Horses for the King.* Harcourt, 1996. **M J**
The Celtic youth Galwyn was forced to work for his uncle, a brutal sea captain, as an interpreter. Galwyn was far more comfortable working with horses and on dry land, as far from the sea as possible. His luck changed when Lord Artos and his companions booked passage on his uncle's ship, headed for the horse fair at Septimania to buy the massive black Libyans Artos needed for his knights if he hoped to defeat the Saxons. After Galwyn helped Artos bargain for the horses and get them safely back to Briton, he was rewarded with a position of trust on the count's horse farm, taking care of his massive stallion Cornix. This is the Celtic Arthur: no Lancelot or Guinevere, just a ruler taking charge, defeating the Saxons, establishing Camelot, but with always time for a kind word for young Galwyn.

203. Morris, Gerald. *The Squire's Tale.* Houghton Mifflin, 1998. **M J**
Raised in the forest by the hermit Trevisant, young Terrance is surprised and delighted to become the knight Gawain's squire. The knight and boy plunge immediately into rollicking adventures, vanquishing enemies (once with a stew pot!) and championing damsels in distress. Along the way, Terrance learns about himself and his background, coming to terms with both the world of chivalry and the world of evil. Fast paced and humorous. Sequels: *The Squire, His*

Knight, and His Lady; *The Savage Damsel and the Dwarf*; *Parsifal's Page*.

204. Paterson, Katherine. *Parzival: The Quest of the Grail Knight.* Lodestar, 1998. **M J**
This slim volume is a masterful retelling of an epic poem that has endured for nearly eight hundred years. Wolfram von Eschenbach, one of the greatest German medieval poets, was also a knight and served several feudal lords before writing *Parzival* in the early part of the thirteenth century. His work was based on stories about the Holy Grail that were well known at that time. In both the German and the English tales of the Round Table, Parzival is a boy raised in the wilderness, totally ignorant of chivalry and King Arthur. Von Eschenbach added the concept of the innocent fool. His Parzival goes through trial, loss of faith, suffering, repentance, and in the end, redemption, becoming the Grail Knight he was destined to be. Parzival's mother did not want her son to die in battle as his father did, so she kept him ignorant of the tenets of chivalry. When some knights tell Parzival of King Arthur and he insists on going to court, she even dresses him like a fool; it doesn't help. After fighting numerous battles, Parzival visits the court of the tormented Fisher King but fails to ask the wounded man what is wrong with him. As a result, Parzival was condemned to roam for years, trying to regain his honor. Patterson's simple, straightforward narrative retelling of von Eschenbach's tale is proof of the lasting power of legends and their impact today.

205. Rice, Robert. *The Last Pendragon.* Walker, 1991. **S**
Mordred (Medraut) had three sons by Elyn, a woman who was also loved by Arthur's knight Bedwyr, the champion entrusted by Arthur to cast his sword, Caliburn, into the lake after Arthur's death. Bedwyr couldn't bring himself to do it and hid the sword in a tree instead. Then the knight wandered for years, consumed with guilt, especially when the sword, recovered by mad king Constantine, was used to kill the two oldest sons of Mordred. The youngest boy, Irion, survived and was raised by his uncle to be a valiant warrior. As a young man, Irion constantly had to fight against the stigmatism of his parentage, despite the fact that he looked more like his grandfather Arthur. When Bedwyr finally returns from Rome in a last-ditch effort to find the sword and carry out Arthur's dying command, he is joined in this quest by the young Irion.

206. Springer, Nancy. *I Am Mordred*. Putnam, 1998. **M J S**
Outcast. Miscreant. Evil child. From the moment of his birth, Mordred was both feared and reviled. Surviving the cruel and heartless death that his father Arthur intended, Mordred forever struggles to find the love and acceptance of parents and family, and he desperately yearns to escape his prophesied fate. Springer has eloquently retold the familiar Arthurian legend of the villain Mordred, making the troubled young man understandable if not sympathetic. A coming-of-age and coming-to-terms story that holds the reader with Mordred's tortured journey to find his true self. Companion novel: *I Am Morgan le Fay*.

207. Stewart, Mary. *The Crystal Cave*. Hodder & Stoughton, 1970. **J S**
Merlin the magician takes the stage in this first of four volumes that depict the rise and fall of King Arthur and the glory days of Camelot. Merlin's mysterious beginnings and the development of his magical powers are vividly brought to life here. Sequels: *The Hollow Hills*; *The Last Enchantment*; *The Wicked Day*.

208. Sutcliff, Rosemary. *The Light Beyond the Forest: The Quest for the Holy Grail*. Dutton, 1980. **M J S**
In a traditional retelling of the Arthurian legends, Sutcliff writes in spellbinding prose of the sword in the stone, Guinevere and Lancelot, and the golden years of Camelot. All the supporting characters have their moments as well—Sir Bors, Sir Percival, the evil Mordred, and others—with the master writer Sutcliff weaving the threads of her tapestry in intricate and brilliant patterns. A saga somewhere between the classic version of Sir Thomas Mallory and the fierce novels of Bernard Cornwell. Sequels: *The Sword and the Circle: King Arthur and the Knights of the Round Table*; *The Road to Camlann: The Death of Arthur*.

209. Wein, Elizabeth. *The Winter Prince*. Simon & Schuster, 1993. **J S**
Lleu and Medraut, half brothers and sons of Artos, are fierce rivals for their father's affection and worldly kingdom. Wein's debut novel is a tale set in an ordinary medieval Britain, a country without the magical Merlin or any lighthearted tales of Camelot. Using the Welsh version of familiar Arthurian names and choosing Medraut (Mordred) as narrator, Wein speaks in a dark and disturbing voice as the half brothers move toward a spellbinding conclusion to their relationship. The cruel Morgause, Medraut's mother, adds a layer of menacing evil. The quintessential story of sibling rivalry.

210. White, T. H. *The Once and Future King*. Putnam, 1971. **J S**
A modern classic of Camelot that begins with the youthful Arthur learning the ways of the world and magic under the tutelage of the wizard Merlin. The tragedy and the ecstasy of his reign are gloriously described as Arthur makes an impact upon his world that continues to this very day. Disney popularized the first book in this lengthy novel, *The Sword and the Stone*, with a highly successful animated version.

211. Woolley, Persia. *Queen of the Summer Stars*. Poseiden Press, 1990. **S**
Again, an Arthurian trilogy, this time told from Guenevere's point of view, a tale that is wrapped in the reality of medieval Britain rather than steeped in magic and blood. Here Guenevere appears a very flawed and realistic woman, caught in a challenging marriage, an all-too-human woman who strives to fit into her place as a ruler's companion. No Merlin, no magic, no dark Celtic paganism: Woolley explores the psyche of an unusual woman of the Middle Ages.
Prequel: *Child of the Northern Spring*. Sequel: *Guenevere: The Legend in Autumn*.

212. Yolen, Jane. *Passager* (Harcourt, 1995); *Hobby* (Harcourt, 1996); *Merlin* (Harcourt, 1997). **M**
Published as separate volumes, these three tales of Merlin's youth function best as a single story. Named for three species of small hawks, Yolen's novels chart the young wizard's progress from forest-raised feral child in *Passager* to the wandering Hobby and finally a return to the woods of the wildfolk, where the dreamer Merlin meets the Cub (Arthur), his companion in future adventures. Short, almost childlike text belies the layers of meaning and nuance in these simple yet poetic retellings. For a bit younger audience than T. A. Barron's Merlin series, this imagery-filled sequence is perfect for young middle schoolers.

A Matter of Belief

Angels, devils, masters of manipulation, self-reliant teens: characters in these novels choose to follow various paths to salvation.

213. Almond, David. *Skellig*. Bantam, Doubleday, Dell, 1999. **M J S**
What's living in the dilapidated garage? When exploring his new home with neighbor Mina, Michael finds an old man. Is he a vagrant? a spiritual being? a menace or an angel? Michael's parents are preoccupied with his baby sister's illness while the young teens are drawn more and more often to the strange being called a skellig.

214. Butler, Octavia E. *The Parable of the Sower*. Four Walls Eight Windows, 1993. **S**
Lauren is a fifteen-year-old African American girl who lives with her family in a walled enclave in California. It is the year 2024, and those inside the walls must be on constant guard against the depredations of those on the outside, in particular be vigilant against the homeless, the thieves, and the druggies. To make matters worse, a new drug, Pyro, has become popular. Pyro is extremely dangerous because it makes starting and watching fires burn a more rewarding experience than having sex. Lauren is a hyperempath, blessed (or cursed) with a gift that enables her to feel both the pleasure and the pain of those around her. When the compound finally falls to attacks from the outside, she is one of the few survivors. Instead of giving up, she leads a small group north, looking for fertile soil, running water, and a secure place in which the remnants of her community, her Earthseed, can take root and flourish. Sequel: *The Parable of the Talents*.

215. Herbert, Brian and Kevin J. Anderson. *Dune: House Atreides*. Bantam Books, 1999. **J S**
This collaboration by the son of Frank Herbert and a best-selling author who first read *Dune* when he was ten is the first in a projected trilogy that goes back decades before the events in that novel. Complex and compelling, this is an account of the youth of Paul Muad'Dib Atreides' father, Leto Atreides, who has to grow up quickly after his mother masterminds the assassination of his father. There is an imperial plot to develop a new source for the spice Melange, vital to the empire and native only to the desert planet Arrakis, commonly known as Dune. The Harkonnen are vicious and treacherous, but the Bene Gesserit witches, involved in a generations-long breeding program designed to produce the Kwisatz Haderach, need both Harkonnen and Atreides donors. After the emperor is assassinated by his son, Leto risks everything to stop a war. Sequel: *Dune: House Harkonnen*.

216. Herbert, Frank. *Dune*. Chilton House, 1965. **S**
This classic epic saga is set in the future on the planet Arrakis, known as Dune, a desert world filled with mile-long sandworms and the immortality drug Spice. Prince Paul is the scion of the Atreides dynasty; he must become warrior and leader to save his dying planet. Herbert creates a complete ecological world on Dune, marrying complex environmental relationships with heart-pounding action. A dark, violent, mesmerizing tale that leaves the reader with unforgettable images of desert battles and royal intrigue. Sequels: *Dune Messiah; Children of Dune; Heretics of Dune; Chapterhouse of Dune*.

217. Kress, Nancy. *Beggars in Spain*. William Morrow, 1993. **S**
Leisha's wealthy father can buy any type of genetic manipulation that he wishes for his daughter. He chooses sleeplessness, which turns her into one of the new elite who never has to waste time sleeping. As a result, Leisha is brighter and happier than her peers, including her own sister. An unexpected side effect of the sleeplessness procedure turns out to be longevity, which heightens the schism that is developing between the sleepers and the sleepless. The book's title comes from a proverb that you can try to give $1 to all the beggars in Spain, but you won't succeed, and they'll still rise against you. Inevitably, humanity finds itself in the role of beggars to the multitalented sleepless. Even the construction of an offplanet sanctuary for this outnumbered elite doesn't remove the threat of open conflict between the haves and have nots. Sequels: *Beggars and Choosers; Beggars Ride*.

218. Levitin, Sonia. *The Cure*. Harcourt Brace, 1999. **M J S**
Gemm 16884 lives in a future world devoid of music, sex, and passion of any variety. The order of this society is based on keeping
everyone calm, tranquil, bland, and anonymous: no individualists
wanted. Gemm 16884, however, dreams of music and singing, and after a series of aberrant behaviors, is given the choice by the elders of
the Cure or death. He chooses the Cure. Gemm becomes Johannes,
son of the Jewish moneylender Menachem, in fourteenth century
Strasbourg. The elders plan that Gemm/Johannes, upon his return to
the future, will forever associate his horrific experiences as a Jew in
medieval France with his love of music and his individuality. Levitin's novel is both science fiction and historical fiction, creating a future society that does not allow people their own religious or spiritual
beliefs and recreating the anti-Semitic society of medieval Europe.

219. Lowry, Lois. *The Giver*. Houghton Mifflin, 1993. **M J**
Jonas lives in a perfect world: There is no disease, all families are
congenial, and each person in this society knows his or her place. On
a child's thirteenth birthday, a public ceremony is held and each adolescent is given a lifetime career assignment. Jonas is passed over during his ceremony; what does that mean? At first fearful, Jonas gradually adjusts to the knowledge that his life's work is to be the Receiver
of his community, the child to whom the Giver imparts knowledge,
wisdom, and the ability to see all the world in a multitude of colors.
The positions of the Receiver and Giver are ones of high esteem, but
they also carry with them the knowledge that all is not perfect in this
futuristic world. Lowry's classic utopia/dystopia novel has received
many accolades, well deserved, and its appeal to teens is as strong as
its literary merits. Companion novel: *Gathering Blue*.

220. Marley, Louise. *The Terrorists of Irustan*. Penguin Putman, 1999. **J S**
The terrorists of Irustan are a group of women who decide to fight
back against the oppressive restrictions of their culture and their world.
Ever since Irustan was settled three centuries ago, men were the only
free ones on the planet. Women must go everywhere heavily veiled.
They are supposedly protected by their fathers, husbands, brothers,
and sons, but in reality, this means that they are at their mercy. A savagely beaten woman has no recourse but to continue to submit to the
abuse until she dies. A woman may not talk to a man or engage in
men's work, and a widow has no way to survive if she has no male relative to care for her. The one profession a woman can follow is that of

a medicant, or healer. That's what Zahra is, using cast-off Earth technology and considerable innate skill. Her husband is the director of the mines, an older man of considerable importance, and he gives her a great deal of freedom in which to follow her profession. But then she decides to get even with those who prey on the helpless, willing to become a martyr to bring about revolutionary changes on her world. A rich, complex work, beautifully written, featuring carefully detailed world building.

221. Russell, Mary Doria. *The Sparrow*. Random House, 1996. **S**
This powerful first novel is by a paleoanthropologist who has written scientific articles on everything from bone biology to cannibalism, a background that she has mined richly for this literate, complex, and challenging work. SETI—Search for Extraterrestrial Intelligence activity—was responsible for a Jesuit missions to Rakhat. The leader and sole survivor of that mission, Jesuit priest Emilio Sandoz, discovers and then loses God because of what happened on the planet. The interstellar songs that called him to Rakhat were beautiful, but the reality of this alien culture was something else. Why did the second expedition to the planet find him in a whorehouse with hideously mutilated hands? Why did he kill the young girl who led the rescuers to him? What happened to his friends and colleagues? These and other questions lead to a Jesuit investigation, during which Emilio recalls the purpose and workings of his quest as well as what happened to him and to the other members of his team. At the same time, he comes to terms with the unbelievable fact that he just might have a future after all. Sequel: *Children of God*.

222. Shinn, Sharon. *Wrapt in Crystal*. Berkley Publishing Group, 1999. **J S**
This author won an award for her first novel, *The Shape-Changer's Wife*, and high praise for her angelic Samaria Trilogy: *Archangel, Jovah's Angel*, and *The Alleluia Files*. Now comes this novel, a top-notch work of science fiction that is also an intriguing mystery and a most satisfying romance. The planet Semay has two religious orders, the dedicated, selfless, hard-working sisters of the Fideles and the vibrant, joyous, empathetic sisters of the Triumphantes. Both are highly regarded and both are stalked by a serial killer who has already sent a half dozen of these sisters to their heavenly reward prematurely. Cowen Drake, special assignment officer for Interfed, has been asked to investigate, not realizing that he would fall in love with one of the potential victims. Impressive world building, in particular the way in

which these two diametrically opposed religious sects support one another, intriguing mystery, and an immensely satisfying resolution.

223. Simmons, Dan. *Hyperion*. Doubleday, 1989. **S**
A group of pilgrims has been selected by the Church of the Shrike to attend the opening of the Tombs of Time on the planet Hyperion. The Hegemony, currently at war with the Ousters, has approved the mission and agreed to provide what support it can. All the pilgrims believe that all except one of their company will be sacrificed to the Shrike. In a manner reminiscent of *The Canterbury Tales*, they all tell their individual stories, with special attention to what in their past lives may have brought them to the attention of the alien Shrike. In the cliff-hanger ending, they go to meet their fate singing, "We're off to meet the Wizard." Sequels: *The Fall of Hyperion*; *Endymion*; *The Rise of Endymion*.

224. Tepper, Sheri S. *Grass*. Bantam, 1990. **S**
A plague is decimating humanity on every planet in the universe except the provincial, isolated world of Grass. Since the planet's authorities refuse to allow scientists in to conduct studies, Marjorie Yrarier, Lady Westriding, is sent as ambassador. A gold medal winner in Olympic equestrian events, she is readily accepted by the planet's upper classes and can join the ruling families as they ride to the hunt. As she conducts her investigation into the strange disappearances and peculiar goings on that occur during this dangerous ritual, she does not realize that her own daughter will be one of the hunt's victims.

Metamorphoses

Characters in these stories either have the ability to change themselves into different creatures—human or animal—or they are metamorphosed against their will. Either way, each must learn to adapt to the unique sensation of being in another's body.

225. Alexander, Lloyd. *The Arkadians*. Dutton, 1995. **M J**
Lucian is a young bean counter in the court of King Bromios of Arkadia. He must flee for his life when he discovers that the royal soothsayers are stealing from the king. During the flight, Lucian meets Fronto, a poet who was turned into a talking ass for drinking from a pool dedicated to the Lady of Wild Things. Fronto asks Lucian to help him find the Lady so that he can beg her to reverse her spell. They are soon joined in this quest by Joy-in-the-Dance, a young girl who, unknown to the two, is also the oracle Woman-Who-Talks-to-Snakes. She was recently consulted by King Bromios, and he was not pleased by her prophecy of "a city in ashes, a king in rags," and now she too is fleeing for her life. The prophecy ultimately comes true, but in true romantic comedy fashion, all's well that ends well.

226. Billingsley, Franny. *The Folk Keeper*. Simon & Schuster, 1999. **M J**
Corinna, disguised as the boy Corin, wishes to become a folk keeper—that person of magical powers who keeps the evil spirits of a house confined to the depths of the cellar. When Corin is offered the position at Marblehaugh Park, she not only has the opportunity to practice her skills but she is able to leave the orphanage and become part of a family household. Once she begins her work, Corinna finds that all is not what it might seem. The folk are very strong at the castle, and taming

them drains her of strength and at times injures her physically. Corinna's relationships with the household's residents are often strained; add to that the fact the Corinna is a selkie—and her longing for the sea increases as the story unfolds. In what may seem like an elementary tale for younger readers, Billingsley adds horror elements that drench this story in details that make it for teen readers, regardless of the large print and short text.

227. Brown, Mary. *Pigs Don't Fly*. Baen, 1994. **S**
Even though Summerdai's mother was the village whore, the obese young girl loved her very much. Now that her mother is dead, she must leave her home and go adventuring on her own. Summer takes with her a dowry she has just found, left by her deceased father, which includes a ring that makes it possible for her to talk to animals. In the course of her journey, she picks up quite a menagerie: a talking dog, a decrepit old horse, a messenger pigeon with a broken wing, a turtle, and wonder of wonders, a flying pig. Appearances can be deceiving, however, as Summer and the dog, Grouch, discover when the true nature of the pig is revealed to them. Sequel: *Master of Many Treasures*; *Dragonne's Eg*.

228. Cooper, Louise. *Sleep of Stone*. Atheneum, 1991. **M J**
Ghysla, the last of the old folk, is a shape-changer. Although her real body is old and monstrously ugly, she can metamorph into any shape she wishes, at any time she chooses, but to stay in another's form requires all her powers of concentration. When Ghysla sees the handsome Prince Anyr and his betrothed, Princess Sivorne, she falls madly in love with the prince and determines to steal Sivorne, hiding her away while Ghysla assumes the princess's beautiful form. In lush, gently paced prose, Cooper spins her magical tale of thwarted love and twisted obsession, beginning the tale at the end. An old man points to a stone in a grotto and relates to two young people the storyteller's legend of the three star-crossed lovers. [Part of the *Dragonflight* series]

229. Cross, Gillian. *Pictures in the Dark*. Holiday House, 1996. **M J**
Charles Wilcox takes on an ambitious project for his school photography club—to photograph the river and all of its various manifestations. While taking pictures, he sees an otter and backtracks it to the house where Peter and Jennifer live. She had just joined the club and seemed to be interested in Charlie. Her younger brother, Peter, however, is a real problem. His bizarre behavior has alienated the other kids at school. Charlie does his best to protect Peter from their cruel

taunts and in the process learns Peter's secret. Another taut page-turner, set in England, by a master of suspense.

230. Cushman, Carolyn. *Witch and Wombat*. Warner, 1994. **J S**
The world of Faerie is the setting for an interactive video game in this novel. Human players are magically transported into Faerie for a tour conducted by the much-put-upon, no-nonsense witch Hali. She only does the job because Bentwood, the troll in charge and self-styled executive producer, has promised her an honest-to-goodness decent witch-type house to replace the International House of Pancakes look-alike she's currently living in. Her familiar is a crow who used to be a man until he made the mistake of trying to pick the witch's pocket. Bernie has become used to being Hali's crow, but now he must change again. Bentwood has convinced Hali that wombats are the in thing right now, and so a wombat Bernie becomes. The four teens they have to take on the tour are a handful, but Hali and her disgruntled familiar are up to the challenge.

231. Hobbs, Will. *Kokopelli's Flute*. Simon & Schuster, 1995. **M J**
Thirteen-year-old Tepary Jones lives on the Seed Farm with his father, who specializes in dryland farming techniques, and mother, who is a noted paleontologist concentrating on the study of old nests, with a special interest in pack rats. She is also trying to solve the mystery of what happened to the ancient Hopi people who disappeared centuries ago. One night, Tepary and his faithful golden retriever, Dusty, make a solitary trip to nearby Hopi remains and encounter a pair of pot hunters. They run away, but the wall they excavated crumbles, and when the mummy of a medicine man falls out, Tepary makes a serious mistake. He picks up the medicine man's bone flute and plays a couple of notes, which activates a shape-changing spell. The first animal Tepary sees afterward is a pack rat, so every night he turns into a pack rat, protected by his faithful dog. Kokopelli himself gets into the act when Tepary's mother comes down with the hantavirus, caused by exposure to infected deer mice droppings, and the boy risks his own life to save his dog in a final confrontation with the pot hunters. In addition to fascinating Hopi and archaeological lore, this is a treat for animal fantasy lovers.

232. James, Mary. *Shoebag*. Scholastic, 1991. **M J**
A cockroach that becomes a boy? And is unhappy about it? James (aka M. E. Kerr) plays metamorphosis for laughs in this lighthearted

spoof. Once the pest becomes the boy, Stuart Bagg, his only desire is to return to his former self, a lowly roach, the son of Drainboard and Under the Toaster. Fellow students at Stuart's school think him rather strange. Add to that Gregor Samsa's torments and Stuart's simpering sister, Pretty Soft, and you have a novel filled with the absurd.

233. Kindl, Patrice. *Owl in Love*. Houghton Mifflin, 1993. **M J**
Campy and offbeat, Kindl's first novel could be described as a metaphor for early adolescence. Heroine Owl at age fourteen craves a mate. Problem: she's fixated on her science teacher, Mr. Lindstrom. Also in the mix is the fact that Owl is a shape-changer; her true form is that of the nocturnal barn owl. Since owls mate for life, her obsession with Mr. Lindstrom gets out of hand. Classmates also think it rather odd that Owl doesn't eat in their presence. To allay their suspicions about her nature, Owl brings a mouse sandwich to the school cafeteria and munches contentedly, carefully concealing any parts that might offend. When Owl discovers the orphan boy, Houle, it is the beginning of her more normal adolescence. Kindl ties up the loose ends of the plot with a satisfying conclusion that allows Owl to be true to her nature—both avian and human.

234. McKillip, Patricia A. *The Book of Atrix Wolfe*. Berkley, 1995. **J S**
Atrix Wolfe is a powerful mage who can take the shape of a white wolf and then live among the wolves in the mountains each year. When the warriors of Kardeth threaten his kingdom, Atrix shapes a dark hunter out of the anger, fear, and despair he finds on the battlefield. What he doesn't realize is that the consort of the Queen of the Wood will be caught in his spell and pulled from Faerie to become the embodiment of the pitiless hunter. Like the queen's consort, the queen's daughter also has some human blood and is caught up in the spell. While the queen is seeking her daughter everywhere, a young child with no knowledge of her prior life is found naked and trembling beside the woodpile at Castle Pelucir. Saro, named for Sorrow's Child, becomes a scullery maid in the castle. She never cries or speaks and only rarely smiles. Recently she has begun seeing visions in her cauldron and is drawn to Talis, younger son of the dead king. Talis, who has been studying magic in the mage school, discovers a magic book and brings it home with him, inadvertently returning the Book of Atrix Wolfe to the scene of so much death and destruction. When the dark hunter follows the book, Atrix Wolfe is summoned to fight him, and the fate of the queen's daughter depends on his victory.

235. Murphy, Shirley Rousseau. *The Catswold Portal*. NAL, 1992. **S**
In his California hillside garden, artist Braden West has an old tool-shed with a door of dark, intricately carved wood. This door leads to the Netherworld below and creatures of the fairy world, including the shape-shifters called the Catswolders. An evil sorceress, Siddonie, has sworn to try to hold power over all the inhabitants of Nether-world; to do so, she needs a child. Siddonie had a child, Sarah, who is now seventeen; now she needs an heir to complete her domination of Netherworld. Sarah does not remember her past—or her time with Siddonie. Above world, she becomes romantically and sexually in-volved with Braden, who initially has no understanding of Sarah's other world form or history.

236. Pierce, Meredith Ann. *The Woman Who Loved Reindeer*. Grove/Atlantic, 1985. **S**
Set in an Arctic-like frozen world, Pierce begins her story when the woman Caribou is given a baby by her sister-in-law. This woman's husband was away during the time she conceived the child. Not only is the infant not her husband's but he is a trangyl—a shape-changer that can take on the form of a golden reindeer. Caribou does raise the baby, and she becomes the wise woman for her tribe. After an earth-quake, Caribou advises the tribe that following the trangyl is the only way to safety, since the man/beast can sort out a path. Hauntingly beautiful, this is one of Pierce's most adult fantasies; it is also a stand-alone novel, not part of any of Pierce's series.

237. Pierce, Tamora. *Emperor Mage*. Simon & Schuster, 1995. **M J**
Book Three of *The Immortals* opens with the young girl Daine accom-panying her mentor, the powerful mage Numair, on a peace delegation to the Emperor Mage of Carthak. Rather than peace, the Emperor Mage wants Daine to use her wild magic to heal the exotic birds in his menagerie. At the same time, he makes plans to capture and execute Numair. If Daine is to save her friend, she must use all of her shape-shifting magic as well as magical animals such as her baby dragon and the monkey she saved from drowning. Daine calls upon the old gods of Carthak to support her in the battle against the Emperor Mage. Pre-quels: *Wild Magic*; *Wolf-Speaker*. Sequel: *Realms of the Gods*.

238. Pullman, Philip. *I Was a Rat!* Alfred A. Knopf, 2000. **M**
It appears that eight-year-old Roger truly was once a rat. He gnaws pencils and fingers, knows nothing of reading, and cannot even sit at

the dinner table without plunging his face into whatever he's eating. Childless Joan and Bob take Roger in when he shows up at their door—and neither doctor, police officer, nor headmaster seem to know what to make of the little boy. After a picaresque set of episodes in which poor Rog is a freak on the lam and back in the sewer, enter Princess Aurelia, formerly Mary Jane, who rescues Roger from a multitude of abuses. This is essentially a tale of the poor orphan returned to love and a good home. Pullman's latest is a romp, played for laughs and skewering everything possible: newspapers in the form of *the Scourge*, a local rag; the royal family; and British public schools.

239. Smith, Sherwood. *Wren's War*. Harcourt, 1995. **M J**
The adventures of Wren and her friends continue in this final volume of a trilogy. Once again the fate of the kingdom is at stake, and Princess Teressa, faced with treachery and the murder of her parents, flees the palace and begins rallying her people against the evil Andreus. At the same time, she must hide from her uncle, who plans to keep her a prisoner and rule as regent in her stead. Connor, her loyal cousin, can help heal the country. But to do so, he must activate the land magic while Wren does some more shape-shifting courtesy of a magic necklace, this time taking the form of a big mountain owl. As far as these young people are concerned, if Andreus wants a war, that is exactly what he will get. Prequels: *Wren's Quest*; *Wren to the Rescue*.

240. Thompson, Kate. *Switchers*. Hyperion, 1998. **M**
Young teens Kevin and Tess have the ability to change into a variety of animal shapes. When a series of snowstorms caused by ice creatures threatens to encase the world in winter, the two teens attempt to battle the Krools and end the descent into an ice age. Sequels: *Midnight's Choice*; *Wild Blood*.

Once Upon a Time

You might recognize these fairy tales—then again, you might not. McKinley and Napoli play with traditional stories, often shaping the narratives into startling new form. Some writers in this category draw from Asian, Middle Eastern, or Russian culture. All are forays into the magical worlds that we've loved since childhood.

241. Alexander, Lloyd. *The Iron Ring*. Dutton, 1997. **M J**
Tamar, the young king of Sundari, risks all on a roll of the dice. His loss means wearing the Iron Ring of servitude, journeying to his mysterious master's kingdom, and trying to regain dharma, honor. Filled with exotic characters—a feisty monkey, a beautiful young goat girl, a garrulous eagle, and warriors and kings—this tale draws on mythology and folk stories with the flavor of India. Part adventure, part tender romance, part mystery, part folklore, *The Iron Ring* is a feast for the mind, a banquet that readers will not soon forget.

242. Card, Orson Scott. *Enchantment: A Classic Fantasy with a Modern Twist*. Ballantine, 1999. **S**
Vanya was ten the first time he saw the sleeping woman lying on a pedestal rising from the center of a lake of leaves. He managed to escape the beast protecting her, and shortly afterward his family left his uncle's farm to immigrate to the United States. Vanya was a young man when he returned to the Carpathian Mountains to awaken the sleeping beauty from her enchantment. To keep the bear guarding her at bay, he proposes marriage and then accompanies her across an ornate bridge to her homeland in ancient Taina. Before he has mastered the language and customs there, Baba Yaga comes for them, and they

must flee for their lives, back across the bridge and into Vanya's world, where Beauty travels on a plane for the first time as she accompanies him to America. Baba Yaga is still on their trail, but all's well that ends well in this lush, lyrical, romantic, absolutely enchanting treatment of a fairy tale staple.

243. Dalkey, Kara. *Little Sister*. Harcourt, 1996. **M J**
Thirteen-year-old Mitsuko is part of the noble Fujiwara family. When the family is attacked, her sister Amiko's husband is killed by warrior monks and Amiko falls into a coma. Mitsuko sets out to search for her brother-in-law's soul, and in her travels, she meets a tengu, a shape-shifting demon, called Goranu. Together Goranu and Mitsuko search the land of the spirits for the wandering soul. Filled with both details of medieval Japanese life and mythical creatures from Japanese legends, this blend of fantasy and history is a meandering tale for younger teens.

244. Doherty, Berlie. *Daughter of the Sea*. Dorling Kindersley, 1997. **M J**
For thirty years, Jannet and her fisherman husband, Munroe, have lived together happily, except for their inability to have a child. One night Munroe comes home from the storm-wracked sea with an infant girl bundled up in his arms. For a year, the couple is blessed with their infant daughter. Then a mysterious stranger appears to Jannet and asks her to give him his daughter. When the stranger sees how happy and well-cared for the baby is, he agrees to let her stay longer and as payment rewards Munroe with a massive catch. Seven years later, when he returns, Jannet again refuses to give up the girl and in the end tragically shoots and kills the selkie father in a desperate effort to keep him away from the girl. The legend of the selkie is brought to life in this lyrical retelling that resonates of tales from Iceland, Scotland, and Ireland.

245. Fletcher, Susan. *Shadow Spinner*. Simon & Schuster, 1998. **M J**
Crippled and an orphan, Marjan lives a hard life in ancient Persia; yet she has an affinity for language and the exotic tales of her culture. In the sultan's harem, Sharazad (Scheherazade) has been spinning her tales for almost one thousand nights. She enlists Marjan to find the ending for one of her stories, helping the young girl to escape the confines of the harem to seek the old man at the bazaar who seems to know the best of tales. Each chapter of Fletcher's novel begins with "Lessons for Life and Storytelling." The lessons and Marjan's voice

convey the power of words in this ancient society, a power that saves a young woman's life and gives Marjan a calling.

246. Friesner, Esther M. *Wishing Season*. Atheneum, 1993. **M J**
Khalid is a bright young genie who makes an incredible blunder on his first assignment. He waits impatiently in his lamp for his first mortal contact, but it is a cat, not a human, that rubs against his lamp. Khalid is so eager that he immediately grants all three wishes—food, clean fur, and a loving home. But when he returns to his master, he is scolded for his mistake and returned to the lamp, this time with a book to study—*Yazid's Guide to Better-Known Mortal Animals*. Haroun, a young merchant fallen on hard times, adopts the cat, and it leads him to the magic lamp. When Haroun rubs the lamp, he finds himself face-to-face with an irritable and overly hasty genie that forgets the all-important "You can't wish for more wishes" clause. So Haroun gets all the wishes he could ever want, and Khalid is permanently trapped in his first assignment, with hilarious results.

247. Gaiman, Neil. *Stardust*. Avon Books, 1998. **J S**
The town of Wall has stood for six hundred years on the edge of the world of Faerie. Guards are posted to keep humans out, except once every nine years, on May Day, when a fair is held in which humans and fairies intermingle. During the Victorian era, Dunstan Thorn came to the fair in search of his heart's desire and met a beautiful black-haired woman. She gave him a snowdrop, and he gave her a baby. Nine months later, this baby was pushed out through a gap in the wall and given to Dunstan to raise. Now this child, Tristran Thorn, is seventeen years old and in love himself with beautiful Victoria Forester. In an effort to win her love, he sneaks into the world of Faerie to bring back a falling star, which must be returned by the May Day fair. Unfortunately, he may miss the deadline, because the star broke her leg falling out of the sky, and a witch is hot on her trail, determined to take her heart for one of her spells. This was an extremely popular graphic novel, reworked by the author into this lovely, lyrical fairy tale.

248. Geras, Adele. *The Tower Room*. Harcourt, 1992. **J S**
In this fairy tale retelling, the story of Rapunzel is set in a girls' boarding school. Megan is the Rapunzel in this story, but she shares her tower room with two other girls, Alice and Bella, who appear as Sleeping Beauty and Snow White in subsequent books. Megan's

parents leave her at the school while they travel abroad. When they die in an accident, Dorothy, an instructor at the school, adopts the young girl. All is well until a year before graduation. Dorothy becomes infatuated with a much younger man and brings him to the school to work as her lab assistant. Megan is only one of many girls who fall for the charming Simon, but in her case, the feeling is reciprocated. When workmen leave a scaffold next to her building, Simon is able to climb up to her room. When Dorothy discovers their affair, the two are cast out of the school and left to fall back on their own minimal resources. Megan is keeping a journal in which she describes her current living conditions as well as what it was like at the school before she was forced to leave. All three girls share their hopes, fears, and concerns in the real world that resonates with the enchantment of its fairy tale parallel. Sequels: *Watching the Roses Grow* (Sleeping Beauty); *Pictures in the Night* (Snow White).

249. Goldman, William. *The Princess Bride.* Amereon, 1976. **J S**
Luscious Buttercup, farm boy Westley, evil Prince Humperdinck of Guilder, and sadistic Count Rugen: these are only some of the characters in Goldman's send-up of "happily ever after" tales with the princess pursued by dastardly villains and saved by her true love. Goldman wrote the book after the movie. This is one of the few tales that is perhaps better served by its visual half, yet it's still a good read.

250. Lackey, Mercedes. *The Black Swan.* Daw Books, 1999. **J S**
Swan Lake is revisited in this fairy tale that features a powerful sorcerer bent on seeking revenge for his wife's untimely death. He traps faithless women and turns them into swans. His daughter, a sorceress-in-training, is far more powerful than she realizes because her father regularly drains her magical abilities for his own use. He puts her in charge of the swan flock, and as a result, she becomes friends with Odette, a highborn, elegant princess who is the noblest of his captives. When Odette falls in love with Prince Siegfried and the sorcerer's plans for the royal couple are discovered, Odette stands up to her father and fights back, clearing the way for true love to win out in the end. Strong characterizations abound in this lyrical, enchanted tale of shape-shifting, sorcery, and love.

251. Lackey, Mercedes. *Firebird.* TOR Books, 1996. **S**
Ilya is the middle son of Tsar Ivan. His father, now on his third wife, pits his sons against one another to keep them from joining forces and

turning against him. As the family scapegoat, Ilya suffers constant abuse but so far has been able to avoid serious injury by playing the fool. When someone steals the tsar's favorite cherries and he demands that his sons find the culprit, it is clever Ilya who manages to thwart the sleep spell and stay up long enough to see the culprit, a gorgeous firebird with the features of a beautiful woman. She flies away but leaves a cherry for Ilya that gives him the gift of understanding animals, which saves his life when his brothers try to kill him. Ilya sets out after the firebird and discovers that he must play the fool again to save his life, this time in the grand palace. Magic, mayhem, and romance abound in a beautifully written retelling of a well-known Russian fairy tale.

252. Lackey, Mercedes. *The Fire Rose*. Baen Books, 1995. **S**
This retelling of Beauty and the Beast is set in 1905 San Francisco, at a time when even a master of earth magic can't keep the ground from shaking. Rose is the Beauty, a glasses-wearing, hard-working, industrious scholar who doesn't think of herself as attractive at all. After her father's death, she accepts a position as governess to the children of a rich recluse. Arriving at his mansion outside San Francisco, however, she discovers no children, no servants, and no visible employer, just a voice through a speaking tube. Jason Cameron, her employer and the Beast, is a firemaster, an adept, an alchemist, and a man who has been trapped in a half-human, half-wolf body. He has hired Rose to read and translate arcane texts that he hopes will help him reverse this transformation spell.

253. Levine, Gail Carson. *Ella Enchanted*. HarperCollins, 1997. **M J**
What if Cinderella's real problem was that she could not disobey a direct command? According to Levine, Ella was cursed from childhood with this affliction, and siblings and controlling adults soon learned how to torment her. How she deals with her problem makes for a delightful reading of a favorite fairy tale.

254. Marillier, Juliet. *Daughter of the Forest. Book One of the Sevenwaters Trilogy*. TOR Books, 2000. **S**
Sorcha is the youngest child of Lord Colum of Sevenwaters. She has six older brothers: Liam, a natural leader; Diarmid, with a passion for adventure; Cormack and Conor, twins with very different callings; Finbar, rebellious and mature for his age and possessed with the gift of sight; and Padriac, young, compassionate, and devoted to the animals

in his care. Their land is under siege from the Britons, but Lord Colum is a fierce, proud leader, invincible until he falls in love with a sorceress and brings her home to take his dead wife's place. The Lady Oonagh seduces Diarmid, destroys Sorcha's beloved herb garden, and brings devastation to the land when she turns the boys into swans. Sorcha manages to escape but must spend years spinning and weaving the barbed, knife-edged starwort to make the shirts that will return her brothers to human form if she maintains complete silence until her task is completed. Sorcha and Finbar had helped a young Briton escape from her father's torture. When his older brother comes looking for him, he finds a beautiful but silent girl instead and takes her home with him. This beautifully written retelling of the fairy tale of the swan brothers is set against a backdrop of druids, fairies, Britons, and Celts and is as compelling as it is satisfying.

255. McCaffrey, Anne. *An Exchange of Gifts*. NAL, 1995. **M J S**
Unhappy at court, Princess Meanne runs away to the little hut in the forest where she spent many happy childhood days. Life in the forest is far more difficult than Meanne expected, especially since she does not know how to clean, cook, or unstop chimneys. In fact, all she knows how to do is use her special gift to grow things, which was scorned at court. Fortunately another runaway shows up at the hut, a young boy who offers to stay and teach her how to live off the land. He doesn't know that she's a princess, and she doesn't know that he's a shape-changer and older than he appears.

256. McKinley, Robin. *Deerskin*. Ace Books, 1993. **S**
In one of her most adult retellings of a traditional fairy tale, McKinley deals with obsessive and incestuous love. The Princess Lissar, image of her dead mother, is raped by her father and flees from further abuse, taking her loyal dog, Ash, into the forest and there giving birth to a child. With the help of the Lady, Lissar becomes a creature of the woods, dressing in white deerskin, her flowing black hair now completely white as well. Her redemption is not accomplished, however, until Lissar returns to civilization and helps a neighboring prince raise a litter of orphaned puppies. The author's lush writing propels this tale. The reader is shocked by the opening scenes of abuse but healed, as Lissar is, by the redemptive process of dealing with a new reality.

257. McKinley, Robin. *Rose Daughter*. Greenwillow, 1997. **M J S**
McKinley has written a version of Beauty and the Beast, this time in

the romantic prose of *Rose Daughter*. The basic elements of the story have changed little: the fall of a wealthy merchant, three daughters who follow him to a poor cottage, a desperate bargain with a Beast, sending young Beauty to live in a magical castle. The difference is in McKinley's language, which has both velvet petals and prickly thorns and is often as convoluted and entwined as the briars in Beauty's garden. This richly textured novel unfolds at a leisurely pace, revealing a surprise ending to a well-loved tale.

258. Napoli, Donna Jo. *Beast*. Simon & Schuster, 2000. **S**
Set in ancient Persia, this Beauty and the Beast tale is shimmering with sensual language, fierce violence, and spiritual awakening. Orasmyn, son of the shah, is cursed by a sorceress pari for allowing an imperfect camel to be sacrificed. He awakes one morning as a lion, a beast that is feared and hunted by the palace staff, including his own father. Beast journeys to India seeking food, sexual partners, and a life outside of the human community, but finds it a lonely existence. Beast returns to his Persian palace, and retrieving his favorite book, carries the sacred Gulistan text to France, where he inhabits an abandoned castle. Beast tends the neglected gardens of his castle, coaxes roses to flourish abundantly, adopts the vixen Chou Chou, and finally arranges for his Belle to join him. As the Beast, Orasmyn can neither speak nor control his animal impulses. In a tale permeated with sensory images of Persia and France, this *Beast* can be both shocking and disturbing.

259. Napoli, Donna Jo. *Sirena*. Scholastic, 1998. **J S**
Mermaids must have the love of a human man to become immortal. Sirena and her sisters sing to the Greek sailors, hoping to shipwreck them and capture their hearts. Sickened by the death of the sailors, Sirena deserts her family and settles on the island of Lemnos. With a twist of fate, the Greek sailor Philoctetes is shipwrecked on Lemnos and Sirena falls passionately in love with him. Napoli explores both eros and agape, the love of the body and the love of the spirit, in this sensuous, romantic tale. What will Sirena give to her beloved, what sacrifices will she make?

260. O'Shea, Pat. *The Hounds of the Morrigan*. Holiday House, 1986. **J M S**
Young Pidge travels to Galway to buy a book. While in the book shop, a beam of light shines on a package, an ancient book that contains the image of a serpent. Thus Pidge sets in motion a lengthy quest, in which he and his five-year-old sister, Brigit, are protected by

Irish heroes and pursued by the evil Morrigan, a shape-shifter that can appear as a hag riding on a motorcycle. Filled with Irish lore and legend, this fantasy is a series of confrontations, escapes, and adventures for the two children.

261. Pattou, Edith. *Hero's Song: The First Song of Eirren*. Harcourt, 1991. **M J**
Inkberrow village is farm country in the land of Eirren, and young Collun is content to be a gardener on his small farm there. When his sister, Nessa, disappears, however, Collun must leave the quiet and safety of the farm to rescue her. Collun and Nessa have a shard of a stone of power, and with help from Brie, a female archer, and the bard Talisen, Collun's journey becomes not only a quest to free his sister but a journey of discovery of his own heritage and strengths. A rousing coming-of-age tale, with literate prose and teen heroes. Sequel: *Fire Arrow*.

262. Scarborough, Elizabeth Ann. *The Godmother*. Ace Books, 1994. **S**
Rose, a conscientious young social worker, wishes for a fairy godmother to heal Seattle's woes. What she gets is Felicity Fortune, irrepressible, kind-hearted, and member in good standing of the Godmothers' Sorority. Felicity helps Rose save several clients, including two young children, the intended victims of a child porno ring. Interwoven within this narrative are familiar fairy tales that have been given a new twist. Puss-in-Boots shows up to help a homeless youth fend off the attack of a Vietnamese street gang. Two children, left by their mother at a shopping mall, succumb to the attraction of a gingerbread house. Snohomish Quantrill, lost in the woods, is pursued by the hit man her stepmom has sent to kill her. This hit man is later forced to switch bodies with a frog. Rose discovers that even magic can't cure society's ills but that people can be helped by compassion and caring, and she has plenty of both. Sequels: *The Godmother's Apprentice; The Godmother's Web*.

263. Sherman, Josepha. *Child of Faerie, Child of Earth*. Walker, 1992. **M J**
Eighteen-year-old Percinet, only son of the queen of Faerie, is in love. The problem is that he is in love with a mortal girl. Being half mortal himself, he is aware of the difficulties. But Percinet assures his mother that the girl has untapped powers and goes off to woo her. Graciosa has been the chatelaine of her father's castle ever since her mother's death years ago. It has been difficult for her, trying to please a cold, heartless man who is only in love with the gold in his treasure room. Things are

about to get much worse, however, for her father has met the unwed owner of a neighboring castle. She is so ugly she is called the toad, but she is wealthy beyond belief. He marries her and Graciosa's life becomes a nightmare until Percinet promises to protect her and whisks her away to Faerie to save her life from her new stepmother. Graciosa still refuses to believe that she has any magical abilities, and because of her sense of responsibility, returns home. This puts her back in the clutches of the new lady of the manor. When Percinet's life is also in danger, Graciosa finally comes to terms with the wild magic within her. This lovely medieval fantasy is romantic from start to finish.

264. Tepper, Sherri. *Beauty*. Doubleday, 1991. **S**
Beginning in a traditional manner, Tepper recounts Beauty's childhood as the duke of Westfaire's daughter, the christening wishes and infamous curse, and the approaching fateful sixteenth birthday. But in this version of the tale, it is Beloved, Beauty's near twin and half sister, who pricks her finger and falls asleep. Beauty, disguised as a peasant boy, escapes the thorny castle, and while tramping the woods, is captured by a camera crew from the twenty-first century—it is recording the last of the fairy world in England. Beauty then enters an overpopulated and ecologically contaminated future in which she is brutally raped. She is constantly seeking a return to her world of 1347 Westfaire, but the search is prolonged by stays in imaginary times and places, including a visit to Hell. Playing with time, a bevy of traditional fairy tales, and fantasy worlds, Tepper has produced one of her most complex and creative novels.

265. Vande Velde, Vivian. *The Rumpelstiltskin Problem*. Houghton Mifflin, 2000. **M J S**
Vande Velde had always found the Rumpelstiltskin tale implausible. None of the plot elements seemed logical to her—or the characters' motivations—so she simply rewrote the story (six times) with the same characters, different tone, and new spin on the plot. Tongue-in-cheek versions, one horror tale, and imaginatively creative adjustments to the straw into gold story make this one of the most entertaining titles in this "Once Upon a Time" chapter.

266. Watt-Evans, Lawrence and Esther M. Friesner. *Split Heirs*. TOR Books, 1994 (pb). **J S**
Fairy tale conventions are stood on their head in this lighthearted romp of a fantasy. The ancient and honorable kingdom of the Hydrangeons

was conquered by the brutal Gorgorians. King Gudge took the Hydrangean heiress to wife, but when she went into labor, she had not one but three babies. Since the Gorgorians believe that a woman who has more than one baby must have slept with more than one man, Artemisia was facing death. Old Ludmilla, Artemisia's faithful nursemaid, was standing by to take the extra babies into the forest to be raised by Artemisia's brother, the Black Weasel, leader of the Hydrangean resistance fighters. Unfortunately, the nurse's eyesight is poor, and she takes the two boys, leaving the only girl behind by mistake. Ludmilla then died en route, so one child is raised by a shepherd and the other was purchased by a wizard and educated in things magical. Since King Gudge has already been informed that he had a son and heir, the boys' sister has to pretend that she is a boy. There's laugh-out-loud humor here, especially when their family reunion involves a battle with a dragon.

Postapocalypse

Through accident or by design, Earth has experienced a cataclysmic nuclear event and all the inhabitants must begin rebuilding a civilization.

267. Brin, David. *The Postman*. Bantam, 1985. **J S**
   Gordon is a survivor of the war that destroyed civilization thirteen years ago. Now he is a traveler, having left the shattered East behind and traveling West. To his surprise, along the way he becomes one of the last upholders of humanity. It all starts when he stumbles upon the body of a dead postman. With the postman's coat, hat, and leather bag in his possession, Gordon is mistaken for an official from the East at his next stop. He goes along with the rumors about the existence of a restored United States back East, but then he is forced into a leadership role as the people he meets expect him to help bring civilization back to the West as well.

268. Butler, Susan. *The Hermit Thrush Sings*. Dorling Kindersley, 1999. **M J**
   At some time in the future, Earth suffers a cataclysmic event, causing much devastation. The remaining humans are herded into scattered villages by the rulers. There are walls, guards, and locked gates, thus isolating one community from another and preventing any communications between enclaves. Leora lives in such a village. She is an adopted child with a strange webbed left hand that identifies her as a genetically altered human. She is in grave danger from Wilfert, the evil son of her host family, and she knows that she must escape. Finding the gate to her community unlocked one day, Leora steps into the forest, encountering a lost birmba baby and returning the creature to its mother. The rulers have always told the villagers that the birmbas

are dangerous and life threatening—one of their lies to enslave the population. Leora journeys to find her sister and along the way finds scattered groups willing to join her in rebelling against the powers that keep them confined.

269. Frank, Pat. *Alas, Babylon*. Buccaneer Books, 1990. **M J S**
In 1959, the author was asked what he thought would happen if the Russians launched a Pearl Harbor–style sneak attack on the United States—this time it would be nuclear bombs that fell out of the skies. Frank replied with an answer that proved to be conservative compared with official forecasts published later: "Oh, I think they'd kill fifty or sixty million Americans—but I think we'd win the war." His questioner then responded that the deaths of fifty or sixty million Americans would create quite a depression. The exact nature and extent of that depression is presented here in what has become a postapocalyptic classic, a riveting account of what happens in one small town after the country is devastated by a nuclear holocaust.

270. McIntyre, Vonda N. *Dream Snake*. Houghton Mifflin, 1978. **J S**
Snake is a healer in a postnuclear holocaust future where tribal groups live in a primitive society and depend on their healers to keep them healthy. She must culture vaccine from her snakes, including a rattlesnake and a cobra, to use when necessary. Most important of all, however, is her dream snake, which she uses to deaden pain and ease death. When this precious snake is killed by the frightened family of one of her young patients, she must go on a seemingly hopeless quest to find a replacement. For without a dream snake, she cannot remain a healer.

271. Miller, Walter. *A Canticle for Leibowitz*. Ultramarine Publishing, 1975. **S**
It is long after Earth has experienced the flame deluge, a cataclysmic nuclear episode, and civilization has returned to a primitive state. A group of holy monks live in an isolated community in the Utah desert, among them Brother Francis of the Albertian Order of Leibowitz. While doing penance outside the monastery walls, Brother Francis discovers the holy relics of the blessed saint himself—a partial blueprint and a shopping list. After the simplification, all questioning and scientific data seemed irrelevant. Brother Francis's discovery returned his isolated order to some prominence in this medieval-like world. Crafted in three sections, Miller explores the effects of the discovery of the relics on three time periods, with the reader aware of the ab-

surdity of worshipping these common twentieth-century documents. Miller presents the theological questions and soul-searching of these monks set against society's withdrawal from valuing scientific evidence. Long a classic of the science fiction genre, *Canticle* is also one of the best. Sequel: *Saint Leibowitz and the Wild Horse Woman*. **S**

272. Murphy, Pat. *The City, Not Long After*. Doubleday, 1989. **S**
A plague has decimated Earth. According to legend, peace would be brought to the world if the monkeys from a monastery in the Himalayas called the Mountain of Peace were taken away. So the monkeys were scattered among all the population centers where the plague virus they bore began to spread. Peace was the result, but not the kind of peace that everyone had expected. One group of survivors, mainly artists, takes over San Francisco, aided by the ghosts in the city. Miles away, Mary Laurenson, one of those who released the monkeys, gives birth to and raises her daughter. Life has not been easy, but they have survived. Then Fourstar and his army arrive, bent on taking over all the cities, including San Francisco. Mary is one of the general's victims, but she manages to send her daughter away on a mission to warn those in San Francisco. As a result, she is adopted by San Francisco, accepted by its ghosts and the misfits living there. She is happy until Fourstar finally arrives and the war begins, with both human and nonhuman inhabitants fighting to protect their city.

273. O'Brien, Robert C. *Z for Zachariah*. Atheneum, 1975. **M J**
After the bombs drop, only sixteen-year-old Ann is left alive in a valley protected by a strange weather inversion that blows the deadly radiation in the opposite direction. When Ann sees a man in a green radiation-proof suit walking across the barren land toward her valley, she thinks of the picture book she used in Sunday school, in which "A is for Adam" meant the first man. Unfortunately her "Z is for Zachariah" (the last man), becomes a deadly threat when he reaches her valley and she discovers just what this victim of radiation poisoning wants of her.

274. Palmer, David R. *Emergence*. Spectra, 1984. **J S**
When germ warfare wipes out all homosapiens on Earth, it is time for the homo posthominem to take over. Eleven-year-old Candy is one of this new breed. When she crawls out of a fallout shelter, Candy discovers that she is one of the few survivors. This is the journal of her search for other survivors so that Earth may be repopulated.

275. Stevermer, Caroline. *River Rats*. Harcourt, 1991. **M J**
For fifteen years after the nuclear holocaust called the flash, the ancient Mississippi steamboat known as the *River Rat* was used as an
orphanage. Then it was liberated by a group of teens that became
River Rats, working their way up and down the polluted Mississippi
River, supporting themselves by delivering mail and giving rock con-
certs along the way. Their only hard and fast rule was not to take on
passengers, and the one time they broke it, they almost lost their boat
and their lives.

276. Stewart, George R. *Earth Abides*. Fawcett, 1971. **J S**
This postapocalyptic disaster novel shows how one person survives
the destruction of civilization. Isherwood Williams was a graduate
student investigating the ecology of humans, plants, and animals in
the mountains of California when a rattlesnake bite saved his life. By
the time he recovered from the venom and returned to civilization,
humankind was virtually extinct, wiped out by a strange disease. Returning to his home in San Francisco, Isherwood found his parents
and almost everyone else gone. Afterward he traveled cross-country
looking for more survivors. Finding only a few people elsewhere, he
returned to San Francisco and started his own tribe.

277. Strieber, Whitley. *Wolf of Shadows*. Alfred A. Knopf, 1987. **J S**
After the bombs drop, nuclear winter arrives. The leader of a wolf
pack understands what this drastic change in the weather means. With
his cubs dying and no food remaining to scavenge, he leads his pack
on the long trek south, allowing a human mother and her daughter to
accompany them.

Space Opera

On a broad and sweeping canvas, these authors play their tales for dramatic effect, oftentimes for laughs, and always with a galactic view.

278. Asprin, Robert. *Phule's Company*. Ace Books, 1990. **J S**
In this humorous spoof of military science fiction, the son of a megamillionaire munitions supplier joins the legion after a fight with his father. When Phule mistakenly strafes a peace conference, he is given a punishment detail—captain of the Omega Company—an outfit noted for its assortment of misfits, criminal types, and overt rebels. The narrator, Phule's ever-present butler, describes how Phule takes command, transforms his new unit into one capable of beating the army's elite Red Eagle unit in war games, and even turns an encounter with hostile aliens into a financial windfall. Sequels: *Phule's Paradise*; *A Phule and His Money*.

279. Bujold, Lois McMaster. *The Warrior's Apprentice*. Baen, 1990. **S**
Miles Vorkosigan is the son of the prime minister of Barrayar, a warlike planet with a strong military hierarchy. Because his pregnant mother was exposed to poison gas, he was born a dwarf with brittle bones but an extremely high IQ. Miles is determined to make it on his own, but when he breaks a leg on the obstacle course at the military academy, he is sent to visit his mother's family on the planet Beta. While trying to be helpful, Miles buys a spaceship, which is against Betan law. He also gets involved in a rebellion and winds up acquiring a mercenary force several thousand strong, which is an offense punishable by death on his home world—and this is only the beginning of Miles' fast-paced, action-filled adventures. Prequels: *Shards of Honor*;

Barrayar. Sequels: *The Vor Game*; *Mirror Dance*; *Cetaganda*; *Komarr*; *A Civil Campaign.*

280. Cherryh, C. J. *Tripoint.* Warner Books, 1995. **S**
The Hugo Award-winning author of *Cyteen* and the Chanur series has written another novel set in her Merchanter universe. Tom Hawkens is a junior tech on the spaceship *Sprite*. His mother, raped by his father, chose to have the baby; but she left Tom in the ship's nursery most of the time. Her visits with him were limited because whenever she felt like hurting him to get even with his father, she would send him away. For more than twenty years she has plotted vengeance against Tom's father, who is now captain of the *Corinthian*. When her plot backfires, it is Tom who is the innocent victim, captured by his half brother and taken aboard the *Corinthian*, which immediately leaves for Tripoint and Pel with the *Sprite* in hot pursuit. Tom expects to be spaced, abandoned, or sold to the highest bidder. Instead, he is given a chance to come to know and respect his father and in the end learns that there are two sides to every story.

281. Feintuch, David. *Midshipman's Hope.* Warner Books, 1994. **S**
Seventeen-year-old Nicholas Seafort is senior midshipman on the spaceship *Hibernia*, bound on a seventeen-month mission to Hope Nation and other ports of call with passengers and needed supplies. The ship has a full complement of line officers when the voyage begins, but a freak accident and illness soon leave Nick in charge. Before journey's end, he must face his own self-doubt and insecurities, stand up to hostile passengers who want him to turn back, and put down a mutiny on a mining colony that almost costs him the ship. The true horror of the voyage comes when amoeba-like aliens attack the *Hibernia*. Sequels: *Challenger's Hope*; *Prisoner's Hope*; *Fisherman's Hope*; *Voices of Hope*; *Patriarch's Hope.*

282. Friedman, Michael Jan. *Reunion. Star Trek: The Next Generation.* Simon & Schuster, 2000. **J S**
This is the first hardcover written for the Star Trek: The Next Generation franchise, and it is a nicely crafted science fiction mystery. The reunion of the title is that of the crewmen who worked with Captain Jean Luc Picard in a former command. They also knew Dr. Crusher's husband and were present when he died, and one of them is finally able to clear up the circumstances surrounding Crusher's death. They have converged on the *Enterprise* because one of their number has to

leave Star Fleet to assume the rule of his world after the death of his father. The *Enterprise* is taking him home, and his former crewmates are going along as his honor guard. All goes well until someone on the *Enterprise* tries to kill him. In the meantime, the ship has been caught in a slipstream in space and is plummeting out of control toward Romulan space. Who will plunge the Federation into interstellar conflict by killing the new heir first: the assassin or a Romulan bird of prey? Space opera at its most diverting—lightweight, fast paced, and fun.

283. Heinlein, Robert A. *Starship Troopers*. G. P. Putnam's Sons, 1976. **J S**
This Hugo Award winner is a classic military adventure involving intense military training, an ongoing patriotic battle against impossible odds, and most of all, incredible alien bugs. This is early Heinlein, so the emphasis here is on patriotic duty, the need to do the right thing, and the military as the savior of mankind. Only retired veterans can vote in this world, which puts a very different face on the meaning of civic duty. Johnny Rico joins the service straight out of high school and becomes a member of the mobile infantry. He survives a particularly grueling stint in basic training, during which he is brutally flogged. In the battles against the bugs, he wears a truly creative invention, a powered armored suit, a mixture of spaceship and tank that can deliver death on a more personal level while protecting the wearer against almost everything. As the war continues, Johnny signs up for officer candidate school, more basic training, only this time among young gentlemen on the fast track for an officer's appointment. Digressions are interwoven to provide the background information as to why he is fighting, the importance of the military, and relationships built on honor and trust. Most memorable are the fast-paced battle scenes against those incredible bugs.

284. Moon, Elizabeth. *Hunting Party*. Baen Publishing, 1993. **S**
Heris Serrano was forced to resign her regular space services commission after a dispute with a bloodthirsty admiral who enjoyed watching his troops die. Her new command, captain of the luxury yacht *Sweet Delight*, is quite a comedown, at least at first. She is to shuttle around its aged owner, Lady Cecelia; whip a mediocre, lackadaisical crew into shape; overhaul the ship; and dismantle the smuggling operation set up by the former captain. Worst of all is having to cope with the royal pains, Lady Cecelia's nephew Ronnie and his five friends. When Ronnie and his friends disappear, Heris finds them on

an island, hunted as prey along with members of her former crew. The hunter is the same admiral who drummed her out of the service, and soon she too is running for her life. Sequels: *Sporting Chance*; *Winning Colors*.

285. Sheffield, Charles and Jerry Pournelle. *Higher Education. A Jupiter Novel*. St. Martin's Press, 1996. **J S**
This is the first in the Jupiter series, original novels that bring back the virtues of classic science fiction such as that that of Heinlein and Asimov for today's teens and include fast-paced adventure, colorful characters, scientific accuracy, and thought-provoking ideas. Sixteen-year-old Rick Luban is expelled from school but given one last chance to make something of himself: he qualifies for training as an asteroid miner. Once Rick gets into space, he discovers that mining is a dangerous profession in and of itself but that corporate espionage can make it even more deadly. Others: *The Billion Dollar Boy*; *Putting Up Roots*; *The Cyborg from Earth* (by Charles Sheffield); *Starswarm* (by Jerry Pournelle); *Outward Bound* (by James P. Hogan).

286. Sherman, Josepha and Susan Shwartz. *Star Trek: Vulcan's Forge*. Simon & Schuster, 1997. **M J S**
While mourning the loss of his friend, Captain James T. Kirk, Captain Spock of the science ship *Intrepid II* must think of helping another friend, David Rabin. Years before, Spock and Rabin battled evil forces on the planet Vulcan. Now Rabin needs Spock to aid him in combating saboteurs on the desert-like planet of Obsidian. Sherman and Shwartz alternate the two friendship stories, paralleling Rabin's and Spock's actions in the past with their present troubles. Appealing even to non-Trekkies, this well-paced science fiction story also contains good character development, creative world building, and non-stop action. Sequel: *Vulcan's Heart*.

287. Thornley, Diann. *Ganwold's Child*. TOR Books, 1995. **J S**
A mother and child flee a Musaki slaver, land on the planet Ganwold, and are given asylum by the natives there. Years later, when the mother develops the coughing sickness, her son, Tristan, accompanied by his best friend, the warrior Pulou, goes to the flat-teeth people (humans), seeking medical help for his mother. Tristan doesn't know it, but his father is a celebrated hero, General Lujan Serege, leader of the special forces of the Unified Worlds. At the spaceport,

Tristan comes to the attention of Governor Mordan Renier, his father's deadliest enemy. Tristan and Pulou are taken offworld by the governor and held as pawns in a deadly game of cat and mouse. Their only chance of survival is the father Tristan hasn't seen since he was two years old. Sequels: *Echoes of Issel*; *Dominion's Reach*.

288. Weber, David. *On Basilisk Station*. Baen Books, 1995. **S**
This is the first in a series dedicated to C. S. Forester and featuring a female officer in the fleet that is the perfect embodiment of Horatio Hornblower. Honor Harrington is truly honorable as well as loyal, persevering, and navy to the core. She is put in command of HMS *Fearless*, a light cruiser that has been gutted to make way for the installation of experimental weaponry. Unfortunately this results in a poor performance in fleet exercises and earns her a punishment detail to Basilisk Station. There she encounters an old enemy from academy days and stops an invasion by the Republic of Haven. This is just the beginning of a series in which a strong female protagonist does the right thing, no matter what. Sequels: *The Honor of the Queen*; *The Short Victorious War*; *Field of Dishonor*; *Flag in Exile*; *Honor Among Enemies*; *In Enemy Hands*; *Echoes of Honor*; *Ashes of Victory*.

289. Zahn, Timothy. *Star Wars: The Last Command*. Bantam Books, 1993. **J S**
Volume Three of a three-book cycle shows Star Wars to be alive and well in the capable hands of an author who is an expert at military science fiction. The action takes place years after the movie *Return of the Jedi*. Luke is looking for the clone of a master Jedi who is working for the empire. A new grand admiral has appeared, and the rebel alliance is on the run again. The Dark Jedi C'baoth has been promised Luke, Leia, and the twins Leia and Han Solo are expecting. Chewie and Lando and those inimitable robots, R2D2 and C3P0, are there to see that the babies are safe. Added to the equation this time is the smuggler Karrde and his apprentice, the former emperor's hand, Mara Jade, who may join the rebel alliance against the empire. It's good vs. evil time again in the struggle for truth and justice. The movie characters come alive, with the same breezy dialogue and crackling, fast-paced action seen on the big screen. Lots of battle scenes, exotic other-world settings, and the nobility and innate goodness of Luke leave the reader cheering for the good guys at the conclusion. Prequels: *Star Wars: Heir to the Empire*; *Star Wars: Dark Force Rising*.

A Story, A Story

These collections are as varied as the fantasy and science fiction genres: they can be filled with technical details, describe imaginary worlds, or present the reader with endearing characters.

290. Asimov, Isaac. *I, Robot*. Gnome Press, 1950. **J S**
This collection of short stories about robots and their relationship with humans first introduces the author's three famous Laws of Robots: 1. A robot may not injure a human being, or through inaction, allow a human being to come to harm. 2. A robot must obey the orders given it by human beings except where such orders would conflict with the First Law. 3. A robot must protect its own existence as long as such protection does not conflict with the First or Second Law.

291. Asimov, Isaac, Martin Greenberg, and Charles Waugh, editors. *Young Extraterrestrials*. Harper & Row, 1984. **M J**
Eleven short stories feature alien children on earth. Some children are obviously nonhuman, whereas others live among human friends with no one the wiser. Whether they are ambassadors of peace or a threat to survival, the stories show what life on Earth is like for these young extraterrestrials.

292. Beagle, Peter. *Giant Bones*. ROC, 1997. **S**
Setting his six short stories in the imaginary world he created in *The Innkeeper's Song*, Beagle weaves these first-person narratives around a legendary bard, a race of gentle giants, an evil queen, a troupe of traveling players, a helpful fish, and two old mercenaries—the only characters featured in *The Innkeeper*. Rich language and an aura of the Brothers Grimm.

293. Bradbury, Ray. *The Martian Chronicles*. Bantam, 1952. **J S**
Gripping stories of the colonization of Mars and what humankind faces as a result. Written in Bradbury's poetic style, there is less of an emphasis on technology here and more on the psychological aspects of humans coping with life on the red planet. By turns lyrical, haunting, and horrific, this collection is acknowledged by many to be the author's greatest work.

294. Bradbury, Ray. *The Illustrated Man*. Doubleday, 1958. **J S**
Eighteen science fiction and fantasy stories are linked by an illustrated man. He is covered with tattoos that come to life and act out stories for an interested bystander—who discovers too late that curiosity really can kill the cat.

295. Bradley, Marion Zimmer. *Towers of Darkover*. DAW, 1993. **J S**
Set on the planet Darkover, the stories in this collection are built around the central theme of the towers. These fortress-like citadels house people gifted with such powerful mental abilities as weather control, long-distance communication without the assistance of technology, defense techniques, and visits to a spectral other world. While their medieval-like society is heavily dependent on mental abilities, these people can still hold their own against the technological marvels of the space-faring Terrans from Earth.

296. Brooke, William. *Untold Tales*. HarperCollins, 1992. **M J**
Reversals abound in these fairy tales turned topsy-turvy: the princess rather likes her gallant frog; Beauty, not the Beast, has problems with her looks; Prince Charming can't talk Sleeping Beauty into one little kiss; and the last tale is being "un" written by the computer, much to author Brooke's dismay. Charming with a bite. Others in the series: *A Telling of the Tales: Five Stories*; *A Teller of Tales*.

297. Coville, Bruce, compiler. *A Glory of Unicorns*. Illustrated by Alex Berenzy. Scholastic, 1998. **M A**
gaggle of geese, a pride of lions, and according to Coville's definition, a glory of unicorns: these soaring stories about the mythical creatures with single horns range from the mysterious to the playful.

298. Donoghue, Emma. *Kissing the Witch: Old Tales in New Skins*. HarperCollins, 1997.**S**
Point of view is the name of the game in these deliciously thought-provoking tales. Each story's female character develops from the

previous narrative, linking the stories together, always with a feminist touch.

299. Galloway, Priscilla. *Truly Grim Tales*. Delacorte Press, 1995. **M J**
Fractured fairy tales that are dark and brooding, with unusual twists and turns. Eight traditional fairy tales have been given untraditional interpretations. Rumpelstiltskin is dealing with his own daughter, the giant Jack sees at the top of the beanstalk has to eat people because he's suffering from a fatal bone disease, Snow White's evil queen stepmother was an abused child whose insecurities are behind her attempt to kill her stepdaughter, and Prince Charming has a foot fetish, which is why he is so attracted to that glass slipper.

300. Goldstein, Lisa. *Travellers in Magic*. TOR Books, 1994. **J S**
This compelling collection, the author's first, is a well-written, lyrical exploration of the appearance of magic in the mundane world. The protagonists come face to face with the strange, the unearthly, and the weird: playing cards that depict the present and foretell the future; a young man who lives his life according to a collection of photographs; a Cinderella who finds that life with Prince Charming is not as happy-ever-after as she expected; a pregnant detective who rescues Demeter for Persephone; even aliens who link the fate of the Earth to the musings of an elderly nursing home inhabitant.

301. Laumer, Keith. *Dangerous Vegetables*. Baen Books, 1998. **S**
Tomatoes—the rogue variety, potatoes—three-foot-tall and slimy, pumpkins, and mushrooms . . . this collection is one delightfully wicked vegetarian feast after another. Mixing both new tales with classic favorites, Laumer's anthology is food for the humorist's soul. Celerarious.

302. Mahy, Margaret. *The Door in the Air and Other Stories*. Illustrated by Diana Catchpole. Delacorte Press, 1991. **M J**
The child Aquilina flies through the air on her trapeze, never setting foot on the ground: will this work when love beckons? Mrs. Baskins bakes a fabulous cake for her son, Brian; it looks too good to eat and is in danger of becoming a work of art instead of a gastronomic treat. Matilda passes the mysterious magician's tower on her way home, climbs the winding staircase, and wonders who lives there. Author Mahy has written a whimsical, sophisticated collection of stories; each startles the imagination.

303. McCaffrey, Anne. *The Girl Who Heard Dragons*. TOR, 1994. **J S**
An eclectic collection of stories that includes an all new Pern
novella, the title story featuring a young girl who keeps her ability to
hear and talk to dragons a secret because this was the only way she
could save her holder family from persecution before being accepted
in a Weyr. Among the other stories are a new brain/brawn adventure
set in the world of *The Ship Who Sang* and a return to the planet
Doona. Music, a futuristic MASH unit, sleep therapy, time travel, artificial insemination, ghosts, the Civil War, and horses appear in the
other tales. Particularly enjoyable is the introductory essay, "So,
You're Anne McCaffrey."

304. McKinley, Robin. *A Knot in the Grain*. William Morrow, 1994. **M J**
Four of the five stories in McKinley's collection are set in her fantasy world of Damar. The title story takes place in contemporary
society and involves the displacement of a home by a superhigh-
way. In the Damar stories, a young mute, Lily, learns midwifery; a
princess must face a terrifying ritual on her name day; strange hap-
penings take place in Touk's garden; and the old farmer and his
young wife, Coral, must deal with Buttercup Hill. A touch of magic
and an atmosphere of the faerie world bind these tales together in
tone and theme.

305. Norton, Andre and Martin Harry Greenberg, editors. *Catfantastic:
Nine Lives and Fifteen Tales*. Daw Books, 1989. **J S**
Calling all feline lovers: these short stories are set in the past, the future, and in fantasy worlds. Clever, humorous, adventurous, and magical: these kitties will entertain the reader for endless hours.

306. Robinson, Kim Stanley. *The Martians*. Bantam Books, 1999. **S**
Written after his trilogy about the settlement of Mars (*Red Mars, Blue
Mars, Green Mars*), these selections run the gamut from a novella to
poetry. The stories are in the same chronological order as the plots of
the novels—choosing who will go, training missions in Antarctica,
exploring Mars, early terra-forming projects, character studies of individual Mars pioneers, and the formation of government rules and
regulations. Suffused with humor, sexuality, and Robinson's exquisite
way with words, the reader almost experiences the full dimensions of
the novels. Although reading the trilogy first will add to the pleasure
of reading the short stories, it isn't a must—these gems can be sam-
pled as their own treasure.

307. Stearns, Michael, editor. *A Wizard's Dozen: Stories of the Fantastic.* Harcourt, 1993. **M J**
A cursing caliph and a princess who kicks butt are two of the thirteen wizards in Stearns's eclectic collection of stories. Running the gamut from playful to sassy, these tales each deal with the power of wizardry and the magic of mages, be they male or female.

308. Vande Velde, Vivian. *Tales of the Brothers Grimm and the Sisters Weird.* Harcourt, 1995. **M J**
These are fractured fairy tales indeed: it's the frog that walks out on the princess; there's a short, all-points bulletin out for the arrest of Goldilocks; the prince doesn't want to marry a girl who is too fussy about that pea under the mattresses; and Hansel and Gretel manage to rid themselves of mothers, step or otherwise. Great fun, with a touch of the bizarre.

309. Williams, Sheila. *The Loch Moose Monster: More Stories from Isaac Asimov's Science Fiction Magazine.* Doubleday, 1993. **M J**
A marvelous collection geared toward a teen audience and showing the infinite possibilities of science fiction. The wide variety of stories includes fighting monsters who have developed on a planet as a result of genetic abnormalities; a journey into a television set; a future in which water is a commodity so scarce that lying about it could get a man lynched; a ghost who plays Shakespeare; a life without robots; a rescue by a wolf/woman; alien visitors to Earth; and a time capsule. These are stories that are memorable as well as fun to read.

310. Yolen, Jane, editor. *2041: Twelve Short Stories about the Future by Top Science Fiction Writers.* Delacorte Press, 1991. **M J**
What will school be like for teens in 2041? Imagine choosing an ear in the morning before school that enhances sounds: your own biological Walkman. Eating swoodies makes you fat so that you can use slimmers to grow thin! These stories present an imaginary future world in which teens still do it their way.

311. Yolen, Jane. *Twelve Impossible Things Before Breakfast.* Harcourt, 1997. **M J**
The title is a play on the words spoken by the White Queen to Alice about needing practice in believing the impossible. These stories crackle with wit, have a splash of the modern, and often present a new perspective on traditional fairy tales. From Tough Alice to Harlyn's garden to the Lost Girls of Neverneverland, these tales are a delight to the senses.

Time Warp

Time travel: mayhap the protagonist chooses to move into a different historical period but often arrives in an era without any idea of making such a leap across the years.

312. Asprin, Robert, and Linda Evans. *Time Scout*. Baen Books, 1995. **S**
Time gates open up unexpectedly and are explored by time scouts, and the information gathered is used to set up tourist routes supervised by time guides. Accurate records are kept of each trip, but the more trips a time scout makes, the greater the risk of shadowing, or meeting him or herself. And since the same person cannot exist at the same time as his or her shadow in the same time line, this causes death by misadventure—no exceptions. This is why the legendary time scout Kit Carson finally hung up his ATL recorder and opened a restaurant instead, the Neo Edo. Then Margo Smith arrives, drop-dead gorgeous, looking much older than she actually is (seventeen), and determined to become the very first female time scout; she only has six months in which to do it. Since Margo turns out to be Kit's granddaughter, it's no surprise that she is finally able to convince him to train her, and Kit's friend Malcolm, a former time scout reduced to being a time guide, is also willing to help her. The stage is set for adolescent rebellion followed by love, flight, and a near fatal accident. Sequels: *Wagers of Sin*; *Ripping Time*.

313. Barron, T. A. *The Ancient One*. Penguin Putnam, 1992. **M J**
This environmental fantasy brings loggers and their need for a job into conflict with a young girl determined to save a newly discovered

valley in a volcano's crater from clear-cutting. The ancient one of the title is the largest and oldest redwood in the valley. As the chain saws are revved up, thirteen-year-old Kate and Jody, the son of one of the loggers, crawl inside the ancient one to hide. Suddenly, they are transported back in time five centuries where their help is needed to save the valley in the past as well as in the present. Prequel: *Heartlight.* Sequel: *The Merlin Effect.*

314. Card, Orson Scott. *Pastwatch: The Redemption of Christopher Columbus*. TOR Books, 1996. **S**
Civilization was fighting a losing battle against the excesses of the present when the researchers at Pastwatch, a time travel agency, discovered that it was possible to do more than simply go back and observe the past. With the invention of the specially designed Tempoview and the TruSite I and II machines, it became possible actually to change the past. However, this would put humanity on an entirely different path, wiping out the present in the process. After careful consideration, the researchers decide it would be worth sacrificing their futures if they could eliminate slavery from the New World. Since the institution of slavery in the Americas seems to have begun with the arrival of Christopher Columbus, they know when, where, and who to approach. The question is, how? This dual narrative presents the life of young Christopher Columbus as he gets ready to make his historic voyage and the efforts of the people at Pastwatch to see that his impact on the New World has a different outcome. This unique approach to time travel features strong, well-developed characters; plausible scientific explanations; and history that has been so thoroughly researched that the author provides a bibliography.

315. Chetwin, Grace. *Collidescope*. Simon & Schuster, 1990. **M J**
Hahn, a humanoid android for hyperspace navigation, is a conservationist whose mission is to protect oxygen-type planets from alien encroachment. Attacked by an enemy while trying to protect the Earth, Hahn lands in Manhattan but flashes back in time before touching down to avoid the wholesale destruction of New York City. When his ship is discovered by sixteen-year-old Sky-Fire-Trail, the Native American youth insists on accompanying him forward in time, where he meets a teenage girl who is worried about the planet's future. It is up to this unlikely trio to save the Earth from an alien takeover when the enemy returns.

316. Cooney, Caroline B. *Both Sides of Time*. Delacorte Press, 1995. **M J**
Annie Lockwood is a romantic. Her boyfriend, who works on cars, is not. But she experiences romance galore when she slips back one hundred years in time while visiting the dilapidated mansion. She witnesses a murder and then falls head over heels in love with the heir to the mansion. Strat falls just as hard for this young hoyden who doesn't act or dress properly. His sister is intrigued, and plain but wealthy cousin Harriet, the one he is supposed to marry, is crushed. His father is furious when Strat dances with Annie and the lecherous Mr. Rowwells is able to get Harriet to agree to marry him instead. Then a servant is found dead, a maid is falsely accused, and Annie runs for her life, right back to the present and a boyfriend she now finds sadly lacking. Broken-hearted at the loss of Strat, she is able to return to the past in time to see the real murderer unveiled. In the end, Annie realizes that she must leave Strat, who must marry Harriet, and return to her own time. Sequels: *Out of Time*; *Prisoner of Time*.

317. Cooper, Susan. *King of Shadows*. Margaret K. McElderry Books, 1999. **M J**
When Nat is selected as part of an all-male acting company that is to play at the New Globe Theatre in present-day London, little does he realize that he will meet the bard himself. Nat falls ill with a fever and wakes to find himself in 1599, not 1999, and a member of Will Shakespeare's company. Details of costumes, staging, and Elizabethan England enrich this time travel tale, and young Nat's search for his own place in either society makes for an unusual identity novel.

318. Dunn, J. R. *Days of Cain*. William Morrow, 1997. **S**
This is a unique time travel novel that pits traditionalists against liberals for the fate of all races on all worlds in the universe. The focal point is World War II, specifically the horrors of the Holocaust. One group from the future has been trying and failing to assassinate Hitler, with Alma Lewin and her followers coming the closest to succeeding. Alma is imprisoned in Auschwitz, where she uses money, modern antibiotics, and her knowledge of what will come to help the inmates. When she is killed trying to help a pregnant Jew escape, her followers come back with a specially designed helicopter and destroy the camp. This causes a continuity crisis that must be averted. It seems that the millions must die in the ovens after all, that the future of humankind rests on such a sacrifice. These are truly the days of Cain as

time travelers visit and observe but do not act until they need to—and
then only to maintain the status quo.

319. Finney, Jack. *Time and Again*. Buccaneer Books, 1995. **S**
If time is a river, how much will a twig dropped into it change the
flow of the past, present, or future? That is what Si Morley wonders
when he is recruited by the federal government for a top-secret project involving time travel. A commercial artist, he travels to New York
City in the winter of 1882 and then brings sketches and photographs
back to the present to prove that he actually made the trip. He also
falls in love while he is in the past, but when he discovers that his
presence has put humankind on the road to Hiroshima, he must act before the present is lost forever. Sequel: *From Time to Time*.

320. Haddix, Margaret Petersen. *Running out of Time*. Simon & Schuster,
1995. **M J**
Jessie Keyser, age thirteen, believes her village exists in the year
1840. When a diphtheria epidemic attacks the community and children are seriously ill, Jessie's mother sends her for medical help.
Jessie then discovers that the real time period is the year 1996 and that
her village has been created by unscrupulous scientists and business
moguls who charge tourists money to secretly watch the activities of
the village. Haddix doesn't tie up all the loose ends in this thought-
provoking novel that asks many questions about the relationship between ethics and research.

321. Hautman, Pete. *Mr. Was*. Simon & Schuster, 1996. **S**
Four journals found floating in an aluminum briefcase in 1952 tell the
story of Jack Lund, a young boy who was almost strangled by his
grandfather in 1893. After his alcoholic father murders his mother,
Jack flees through a door that takes him fifty years into the past. There
he meets and falls in love with a young girl who later marries his best
friend. Years later that friend, eaten up with jealousy, leaves Jack for
dead in a cave on Guadalcanal during World War II. Jack recovers and
continues his hopeless mission of trying to go back in time and save
his mother's life.

322. Kimmel, Elizabeth Cody. *In the Stone Circle*. Scholastic, 1998. **M J**
Fourteen-year-old Cristyn isn't very happy about having to spend the
summer with her professor father in Wales. When Cristyn arrives,
she's even more dismayed by the primitive old stone house that her
father is sharing with Erica Dunham, a colleague, and Erica's two

children, Miranda and Dennis. Kimmel weaves the history of the house, the appearance of a thirteenth-century princess, Cristyn's loss of her mother, and the two families' adjustment problems into a suspenseful ghost story with just the right amount of "teens searching for their identity."

323. L'Engle, Madeline. *A Wrinkle in Time*. Ariel Books, 1962. **M**
This classic Newbery winner is still a popular read; L'Engle sends Meg Murray, her friend Calvin, and her little brother, Charles Wallace out into the universe to rescue her scientist father. The children travel by means of the tesseract, or a wrinkle in time, and must face evil forces of the universe. Sequels: *A Wind in the Door*; *A Swiftly Tilting Planet*.

324. Lindbergh, Anne. *Nick of Time*. Little, Brown, 1995. **M J**
Jericho is a student at Mending Wall, a small boarding school that encourages independence and creative thinking. He and his friends are startled one day by the sudden appearance of a new boy in the school. Nick walks out of the kitchen wall and tells them that he is from the future. In his time, their school is a monument, a regular site for tours and lectures on what life was like in the "good old days." Nick invites his new friends to his home for a visit, but when they arrive, they discover that the future is not at all what they had expected.

325. Mason, Lisa. *Summer of Love*. Bantam Books, 1994. **S**
The Summer of Love in Haight-Ashbury is from June 21 to September 4, 1967. Susan Stein comes to San Francisco that summer, wearing flowers in her hair and running away from her upper-class, straight-laced parents. This is her attempt to make a statement about personal freedom and independence. However, researchers in the future know that the 1960s is not only marked by drugs, sex, and rebellion against the government but is also the time in which a major figure in society's future will be conceived. The health of this fetus is so important that Chiron is sent back into the past to protect it and its mother, who happens to be Susan. He knows all about the Grandfather Principle, which means that he doesn't have to worry about murdering his grandfather or he wouldn't have been born in the first place. What he doesn't know is that it was possible to get an abortion in the 1960s. Companion novel: *The Golden Nineties*.

326. Norton, Andre and P. M. Griffin. *Firehand*. TOR Books, 1994. **J S**
In this latest Time Traders novel, Ross Murdoch, an angry young man

who is a valuable member of the Time Patrol team, has received a new name—Firehand. He and weapons specialist Eveleen Riordan have fallen in love with each other and with the planet Dominion. Their mission is to try and avert a tragedy in the planet's past by helping the populace fight a guerrilla war against aggressors. Prequels: *The Time Traders*; *Galactic Derelict*; *The Defiant Agents*; *Key out of Time*.

327. Silverberg, Robert. *Letters from Atlantis*. Simon & Schuster, 1990. **J S**
This entry in the *Dragonflight* fantasy series uses the time travel theme to explore the mystery of Atlantis. Each of its twelve chapters is a letter written by Roy, a time traveler who has entered the mind of the crown prince of Atlantis. The island of Atlantis is warm even during an ice age, and Roy is so intrigued by the alien civilization he has uncovered that he breaks the rules and reveals his identity to the young prince. Roy's efforts to help him save his people are doomed, however, by the fatalistic attitude of the populace in general.

328. Sleator, William. *Strange Attractors*. Dutton, 1991. **M J**
Max wakes up one morning and discovers that he has lost an entire day. He visited a science lab the day before and came home with a phaser that turned out to be a time travel device. A scientist and his daughter want this device back, as do their time traveling twins. Max encounters both sets of twins and falls under the spell of the copy's daughter. Fortunately for him, she feels the same way and stands up to her father when he tries to get rid of Max. The strange attractors here are the people that Max meets as well as the scientific theories involved in the splitting of time lines that could lead to chaos.

329. Wells, H. G. *The Time Machine*. Holt, 1895. **M J S**
The time traveler tells of his adventures in time, proof positive that his machine actually works. He went forward to an idyllic, peaceful world in which the Eloi seemed to have everything they could possibly want. Then he discovered their dark secret involving the cannibalistic Morlocks and had to flee for his life. This time he went so far forward that he literally walked the sands of a dying Earth. This beautifully written classic is acclaimed by many to be the author's masterpiece.

330. Willis, Connie. *Doomsday Book*. Bantam Books, 1992. **S**
Kivrin, a young historical researcher in a futuristic London, is delighted when she is given the opportunity to travel back in time to

visit the Middle Ages. Her goal is the year 1320, but the technician calibrating the time drop is in the early stages of an influenza that will soon reach epidemic proportions in London. As a result, Kivrin arrives near Oxford in 1348, the same year that the Black Death reached England. Although she is soon fighting the influenza herself, she is taken in by a family of nobles fleeing from the Black Death. Meanwhile, her tutor in modern-day London is facing seemingly impossible obstacles in his efforts to rescue her. The city has been placed under quarantine, and the acting chief of the history project has turned off the machinery needed to bring Kivrin back. Companion Novel: *To Say Nothing of the Dog, or How We Found the Bishop's Bird Stump at Last.*

To a Galaxy, Far, Far Away

To travel the stars, visit new planets, savor new civilizations: this is the stuff of science fiction readers' dreams.

331. Adams, Douglas. *The Hitchhiker's Guide to the Galaxy*. Crown Publishing, 1980. **J S**
One moment Arthur Dent is lying down in front of the bulldozers that have come to destroy his house and make room for a traffic bypass. The next he is hitchhiking through the galaxy with his friend Ford Prefect. It turns out he is not human but is a citizen of Betelgeuse, stranded on Earth for the past fifteen years. By profession, Ford is a writer for *The Hitchhiker's Guide to the Galaxy*, so he has the connections that enable him to whisk Arthur away from the doomed Earth just in time. Like his house, the Earth was destroyed to make room for an express bypass in space—which is how Arthur winds up joining Ford on an absolutely zany hitchhiking trip. Sequels: *The Restaurant at the End of the Universe*; *Life, the Universe and Everything; So Long, and Thanks for All the Fish; Mostly Harmless*.

332. Anthony, Piers. *Ghost*. TOR Books, 1986. **S**
During his leave on Earth, Captain Shetland is mobbed by an angry populace who accuse him of being an energy-wasting spacer. Shortly afterward, his leave is canceled, not because of the attack but because he is needed to captain a new spaceship prototype. This is a time traveling vehicle designed to search for new sources of energy desperately needed by a resource-starved, overpopulated Earth. A similar time travel ship disappeared on this same mission, and when Shetland hits a black hole, he discovers why. The ship and its crew are dissipated,

but in their new form as ghosts, they may be able to find the solution to Earth's problems that lies somewhere beyond the end of time.

333. Barnes, John. *Orbital Resonance*. TOR Books, 1991. **S**
Melpomene Murphy belongs to a group of adolescents born and raised on the *Flying Dutchman*, a space colony established after civilization on Earth disintegrated. Collapse was inevitable after MUTAIDS wiped out a large percentage of the population and pollution became rampant. Mel is asked by her instructor on the *Flying Dutchman* to write a book describing the past year on the shuttle in which the older generation, including the parents of all the kids on board, comes face to face with the new, and Mel discovers that she and her friends had been carefully designed and conditioned from birth to carry out a master plan. The children were never told what that plan was—until now.

334. Bear, Greg. *Anvil of Stars*. Warner Books, 1992. **S**
A spaceship sets out to find and destroy the civilization that made and launched the planet-killing machines responsible for the destruction of humankind's home world. The crew selected for this mission is a group of teenagers who come out of deep sleep each time a likely solar system is located. Working together, their mission is to investigate each new solar system, judge its guilt or innocence, and if necessary carry out a sentence of death on the guilty world. As the journey continues, they are joined by an alien ship on the same quest at the same time that a growing number of pacifists on board want to abort the mission. Prequel: *The Forge of God*.

335. Card, Orson Scott. *Homecoming. Vol. 1: The Memory of Earth*. TOR, 1992. **S**
The oversoul, master computer of the planet Harmony, is losing power and can no longer control the planet's inhabitants as it did before. Afraid that a population left unattended will destroy itself as the people on Earth did so long ago, the computer needs to return to the keeper on Earth for repairs. To do so, it must first seek out those individuals on Harmony who are still receptive to its messages and prepare them for the long trek home, a journey and a quest that will take five books to complete. In this first volume, Nafai, youngest son of a wealthy merchant and a respected teacher, is the one who picks up the message sent by the oversoul. Nafai's challenge is to lead his unwilling family and certain other individuals into a future that he has only seen in his dreams. Sequels: *Vol. 2: The Call of Earth*; *Vol. 3: The Ships of Earth*; *Vol. 4: Earthfall*; *Vol. 5: Earthborn*.

336. Hawke, Simon. *The Whims of Creation*. Warner, 1995. **S**
The space ark *Agamemmnon* is on a generations-long voyage look-ing for habitable worlds to colonize. The crew has developed a per-fect ecosystem and a stable, noncompetitive society that is so boring some members are beginning to commit suicide. Then an environ-mental scientist discovers that the plants in the hydroponics garden are being eaten by tiny golden fairies. Shortly after that, three school children enter a virtual reality simulation that was supposed to be ed-ucational but instead involves them in a fantasy quest. The lady in white in the program turns out to be Dr. Penelope Seldon, a scientist in the first generation on board the ship who was forced to go to counseling after she complained that the closed society, with its careful genetic control of future generations, simply would not work and would lead to depression and suicide. That is happening now, but luckily she left an artificial intelligence program for her descen-dants, hoping to wake them up in time. This does not happen until a dozen children disappear, followed by the appearance on board the ship of fairies, elves, unicorns, dwarves, and even a dragon. A won-derful blend of science fiction and fantasy that provides a unique so-lution to the problem of ennui and social decline to a society lacking in creativity and individuality.

337. Lawrence, Louise. *Calling B for Butterfly*. HarperCollins, 1982. **M J**
When an asteroid smashes into the spaceship *Sky Rider*, twelve hun-dred passengers en route to Omega Five are killed. The only survivors are four teenagers, a hyperactive three-year-old girl, and her five-month-old baby brother. These young people, strangers when the voy-age began, argue, bicker, and have temper tantrums. All of this hides their desperate fear as the lifeboat they are in accompanies the dead ship on a collision course with Jupiter. They finally manage to contact a base on Ganymede, but it will take a miracle to save them.

338. Norton, Andre and P. M. Griffin. *Redline the Stars: A New Adventure of the Solar Queen*. TOR Books, 1994. **J S**
Rael Cofort's brother is a major competitor of the merchant trader the *Solar Queen*. Determined to show her brother that she is not a jinx and can make it on her own, she joins the crew of the *Queen* for the flight to Canuche. Nothing out of the ordinary happens until they reach port, but then the aura of menace surrounding the planet be-comes all too real. Before long, Rael gets involved in a shanghai, in-volving packs of rats, and in an explosion at a warehouse—and that

is only the beginning. Prequels: *Sargasso of Space*; *Plague Ship*; *Voodoo Planet*; *Postmarked the Stars*.

339. Pohl, Frederik. *Gateway. Heechee Saga Series. Book One.* Gollancz, 1977. **S**
    Gateway can be the door to unimaginable wealth or to horrors beyond belief. Bob Broadhead, a prospector who thought he had the answer, risked his life by flying out of Gateway on the Heechee spacecraft. Three missions later, he was rich and famous, but now he was Robinette instead of Bob, changed by his trips on the Heechee spacecraft. In the end, Broadhead has to face what happened and what he has become as a result. Sequels: *Beyond the Blue Event Horizon*; *Heechee Rendezvous*; *The Annals of the Heechee*.

340. Sargent, Pamela. *Earthseed.* HarperCollins, 1983. **M J**
    Zoheret is a natural born leader among the children, the earthseed that the ship is carrying. She's the one with sufficient skill to lead her group to victory in the competitions set up by the ship, and when strangers suddenly appear, she's the one who discovers who they are and why they are there. Zoheret even agrees to the war against the dictatorial adults on board so that the children can complete their mission and become earthseed on the planet selected by the ship. After the landing, the children are shocked that the ship will not stay with them. It must go on to seed other planets—after all, everyone has to grow up some time.

341. Silverberg, Robert. *Starborne.* Bantam Books, 1996. **S**
    The Earth is peaceful, if a bit in stasis in the twenty-third century. Consequently, an expedition is sent on a mission to find and colonize a new world. There are fifty scientists on the search ship, *Wotan*, and as they travel through space and nospace—a spatial wrinkle—the sojourners pass the time with games, reading, love affairs, and scientific study. Contact is maintained with Earth through one of the passengers, a blind telepath named Noelle able to communicate with her twin sister, Yvonne, across vast expanses of space and time. Noelle's abilities also include evaluating the suitability of new planets for human life, so she is the *Wotan's* key to both past and future. When Noelle's contact with Earth is mysteriously broken, the ship's passengers fear that they will aimlessly wander the universe and die a lonely death. Silverberg's quiet novel gradually builds the reader's curiosity about what is really happening in this breathtakingly beautiful story.

To Be Continued . . .

We do love a story that goes on . . . and on . . . and on, don't we?

342. Alexander, Lloyd. *The Chronicles of Prydain*: *The Book of Three* (Holt, 1964); *The Black Cauldron* (Holt, 1965); *The Castle of Llyr* (Holt, 1966); *Taran Wanderer* (Holt, 1967); *The High King* (Holt, 1968). **M J**
Based on Welsh legends from the Mabinogion, Alexander's five-book saga begins in *The Book of Three* with young Taran, an assistant pig keeper longing to become a warrior. When his charge, Hen Wen, bolts sorcerer Dalben's caer, Taran follows. Then he meets the knight Gwydion in the forest as well as Gurgi, a munchy-crunchy creature; Dori, the dwarf; Fflewddur Flam, the wandering bard; and, eventually, the Princess Eilonwy. Gwydion and the knights of Prydain are battling the horned king and the evil sorceress, Achren, for control of the kingdom. Taran becomes part of the long war between the forces of good and evil and also searches for his own identity. Occasionally lighthearted and humorous, this engaging saga is filled with intriguing characters, dark scenes of power, and fast-paced action. Newbery Medal: *The High King*. Best read in sequence.

343. Asimov, Isaac. *Foundation*. Gnome Press, 1951. **M J S**
The first volume in the famed Foundation trilogy is still acknowledged a science fiction classic. An ambitious, complex history of the decline and fall of the galactic empire, loosely based on Gibbons's *Decline and Fall of the Roman Empire*, is told in a brief, episodic format. The difference between Rome and the galactic empire is the presence of Hari Seldon. The inventor of psychohistory, Hari has

foreseen everything that is going to happen in the future. This enables him to take certain steps and make the necessary contingency plans for the preservation of human civilization. Sequels: *Foundation and Empire*; *Second Foundation*; *Foundation's Edge*; *Foundation and Earth*; *Forward the Foundation*; *Prelude to Foundation*; *Foundation's Fear* (by Gregory Benford); *Foundation and Chaos* (by Greg Bear); *Foundation's Triumph* (by David Brin).

344. Brooks, Terry. *The Sword of Shannara*. Ballantine Books, 1977. **M J S** Brooks's lengthy Shannara novels somewhat resemble Tolkien's Middle Earth tales, with more emphasis on the picaresque adventures of hero Shea Ohmsford and less philosophical/allegorical connections: this series is simply action oriented. In the first Shannara book, the wars of the ancient evil have ruined the world, and Shea Ohmsford of Shady Vale must wield the sword of power to vanquish the evil warlord. Gnomes, dwarfs, trolls, elves, and talismans of power are introduced throughout the epic narrative. Writing with the flavor of medieval times, Brooks captures the reader with his large cast of characters and his hero's series of exploits. Sequels: (among others) *The Elfstones of Shannara*; *The Wishsong of Shannara*.

345. Cooper, Susan. *The Dark Is Rising*. Simon & Schuster, 1977. **M J** Although this series begins chronologically with *Over Sea, Under Stone*, most readers find the second volume, Newbery-winner *The Dark Is Rising*, first and backtrack to the less exciting first story in the set. *The Dark Is Rising* puts eleven-year-old Will Stanton center stage. The seventh son of a seventh son, Will is one of the old ones who must battle the forces of the dark in the universe. Along with the elderly Merriman and the lady, Will joins with the creatures of the light to find the six magical signs of power and to stand against the dark. Wrapped in images of ice and snow and traveling through time and space, this powerful classic draws on Welsh and Arthurian legends, captivating the reader totally with its poetic language and complex plot. The sequence: *Over Sea, Under Stone*; *The Dark Is Rising*; *Greenwitch*; *The Grey King* (Newbery Medal); *The Silver on the Tree*.

346. Eddings, David. *Domes of Fire. Book One of the Tamuli*. Ballantine Books, 1992. **M J S**
Domes of Fire continues the adventures of Sparhawk, redoubtable warrior and hero of the author's previous trilogy, the Elenium. A six-page prologue succinctly refines more than a thousand pages of text

from the earlier works, leading up to the opening scenes of the Tamuli. Once again there is unrest in the kingdom and Sparhawk suspects that he has not seen the last of the troll gods after all. When a request for help from the emperor of Tamul arrives, the warrior agrees to go to that fabled kingdom, accompanied by Queen Ehlana and their six-year-old daughter, Danae, who is the reincarnation of the child-goddess, Aphrael, with all of her powers. Old friends and foes meet again to battle ancient warriors returned to life, bent only on carnage. The cliff-hanger ending leaves Sparhawk with the seemingly impossible task of saving his kingdom by raising the fabulous Bhelliom from its watery grave. Sequels: *The Shining Ones*; *The Hidden City*. Prequels: *The Elenium: The Diamond Throne*; *The Ruby Knight*; *The Sapphire Rose*.

347. Jordan, Robert. *The Eye of the World. Book I of the Wheel of Time*. TOR Books, 1990. **J S**
It's ten years (Book I was published in 1990) and nine books, and Jordan is still writing this massive, complex series. Not best read in order but MUST read in order, since few readers could pick up (or become interested in) this convoluted, panoramic epic or the entangled cast of thousands without starting at the beginning. And yet, despite the year or so intervals between titles, the new Jordan shoots to the top of the best-seller list shortly after publication, so none of this bothers the legions of readers who anxiously await the next installment. The plot and the players: The Dark One and his minions have been imprisoned following a cataclysmic war. Following this time, men no longer had the ability to channel (it drives them mad to use magic). There are women, however, called Aes Sedai, who wield powerful channeling abilities, and these witches are greatly feared. Myth has it that one day the great male hero, the Dragon Reborn, the reincarnation of hero Lews Therin, will appear to deal with the rumblings of the Dark One. Hero Rand al'Thor and his two companions, Matt and Perrin, begin their long struggle with the agents of the Dark One who have escaped the seals of prison and are about the land, inciting all to choose to serve the evil lord. Rand is the Dragon, but his path to consolidating the factions, kings, and kingdoms of the world is a lengthy and torturous one. There are several romances, including Rand's own love interests, and each book ends with a cliff-hanging scene that makes readers yearn for the next volume. The series to date: *The Eye of the World*; *The Great Hunt*; *The Dragon Reborn*;

The Shadow Rising; *The Fires of Heaven*; *Lord of Chaos*; *A Crown of Swords*; *The Path of Daggers*; *Winter's Heart*.

348. Lewis, C. S. *The Lion, the Witch, and the Wardrobe*. G. Bles, 1950. **M**
Not only for children, Lewis's stories about the fantasy land of Narnia can be read as Christian allegory as well as be enjoyed as tales of magical creatures and time travel. In this first classic tale, four British children—Peter, Susan, Edmund, and Lucy—are spending the years of the World War II at an old house in the country. The youngest, Lucy, hides in a wardrobe one day and finds her way to another world, the land of Narnia, where the white witch has made it always winter and never Christmas. Once all the four children believe in and visit Narnia, they meet fauns, dwarfs, talking animals, and the evil queen herself. The majestic lion, Aslan, helps the children and all the creatures of Narnia to rid themselves of the monstrous evil witch. Lewis's enchanting writing and the perfect pacing of this story make it a smashing read aloud. As the series continues, each book is more complex and has a more demanding reading level, so younger teens who only know *The Lion* could easily be captivated by the rest of the tales. Best to read the first book first, and *The Last Battle* last; in between, teens often read the novels in any order. Sequels: *Prince Caspian*; *The Voyage of the Dawn Treader*; *The Magician's Nephew*; *The Horse and His Boy*; *The Silver Chair*; *The Last Battle*.

349. Robb, J. D. *Loyalty in Death*. Berkley Books, 1999. **S**
This is the ninth in a mystery/science fiction series set in 2059 and featuring New York City cop Eve Dallas and her husband, Rourke, one of the wealthiest businessmen in and out of this world. She's a lieutenant; he has a criminal background: a match made in heaven. In fact, they first met because he was a suspect in a murder case that he later helped her solve. Adjusting to married life hasn't been easy for Eve, who has fallen into the lap of luxury and doesn't have a clue as to how to cope with it, and it is even harder for Rourke, who has to watch his wife risk her life on a daily basis and try not to interfere. This time a terrorist group has targeted NYC for a special demonstration, and Eve is a worthy opponent. Bombs go off; the number of victims rises, including one of Eve's friends; and to make matters worse, the wealthy Branson family appears to be involved. Snappy dialogue, explicit love scenes, fast-paced action, and an intriguing and complex mystery draw all the various plot lines together in this compelling page-turner. Prequels: *Naked in Death*; *Glory in Death*; *Immortal in*

Death; *Rapture in Death*; *Ceremony in Death*; *Vengeance in Death*; *Holiday in Death*; *Conspiracy in Death*. Sequel: *Witness in Death*.

350. Weis, Margaret and Tracy Hickman. *Dragon Wing: The Death Gate Cycle. Vol. 1.* Bantam, Doubleday, Dell 1990. **J S**
Hugh the Hand is an assassin rescued from execution when battle dragons drop from the sky and take him to King Stephen. In return for his life, the king orders Hugh to murder his ten-year-old son, Prince Bane, claiming that Bane is a changeling, actually the son of the evil mysteriarch Sinistrad. Although he is just a boy, Bane shows that he is Hugh's match, willing to use even murder to get his way. What neither realizes is that the boy's klutzy servant, Alfred, is actually a sartan, a servant of the gods who has returned to this world to observe the struggle going on between elves and humans. But will his presence provide some protection against the new menace stirring in the Death Gate? Sequels: *Elven Star*; *Fire Sea*; *Serpent Mage*; *The Hand of Chaos*; *Into the Labyrinth*; *The Seventh Gate*.

Author and Title Index

Note: Numbers refer to entry numbers, not page numbers.

About the Authors

Bonnie Kunzel is a teen specialist at Princeton Public Library in Mercer County, New Jersey, and is vice president/president-elect of YALSA (Young Adult Library Services Association) of the American Library Association. A graduate of Rutgers University, she loves to read and talk about books. Kunzel presents several Best Books programs around the state each year, including Rutgers University's annual Best of the Best in young adult literature, the Spring Conference for the New Jersey Library Association, and the Fall Conference for the Educational Media Association of New Jersey.

Suzanne Manczuk is adjunct professor at Rutgers University, School of Communication, Information, and Library Studies. She is also associate reviews editor for Linworth Publications.